F
CAM

Cameron, Peter

Andorra

$23.00

DATE			

FARRAR
STRAUS
GIROUX

ANDORRA

ANDORRA

PETER

CAMERON

FARRAR STRAUS GIROUX

NEW YORK

LIBRARY OF CONGRESS CATALOGING-IN-PUBLICATION DATA
Cameron, Peter.
   Andorra / Peter Cameron.
      p.   cm.
   ISBN 0-374-10505-7 (alk. paper)
   I. Title.
   PS3553.A4344A83   1997
   813'.54—dc20   96-27928
                                                        CIP

The author wishes to express his gratitude to
Norberto Bogard, Andrew Cameron, John Glusman,
James Harms, Sheila McCullough, Irene Skolnick, Edward Swift, the MacDowell Colony,
and the Corporation of Yaddo.

FOR

VICTORIA

AND

SHEILA

AND

MIRANDA

PART ONE

THE HOTEL EXCELSIOR

> *Even from the simplest, the most*
> *realistic point of view, the coun-*
> *tries which we long for occupy,*
> *at any given moment, a far*
> *larger place in our actual life*
> *than the country in which we*
> *happen to be.*
>
> —MARCEL PROUST, *Swann's Way*

CHAPTER ONE

MANY YEARS AGO I READ A BOOK THAT WAS SET IN ANDORRA and it introduced to me a notion of that country that remained in my mind, so that when I was compelled by circumstances to begin my life again in some new place, I knew immediately where I wanted to go. And it was not difficult to get there, the world being how it is these days, and I went; I left behind all that I needed to leave behind. Which is to say everything. It is remarkable, the ease with which one can change one's life, if one wants, or needs, to.

Yet of course I didn't actually change my life. I am living the same life, only in a different country: Andorra.

Andorra's dramatic topography makes it unapproachable by air, so I arrived via train from Paris, having flown that far. As a general rule—and I am afraid I am the kind of person who believes in general rules—I like to arrive in new places by train. There is something about literally crossing borders, traversing frontiers, watching the countryside hurtle by the window and become exurban, and then the gradual diminution of speed as the train approaches a city, that allows one to arrive with an experience of place that flying disallows.

Andorra is a small country and her city—for there is only one: the capital, La Plata—is proportionately small. The train station at which I found myself was not the chaotic grand temple one expects in European cities, but simply several glass-roofed platforms separated by as many tracks, a whitewashed waiting room with worn wicker furniture and a ceiling fan that rotated at a speed that succeeded only in proving that it was operational. I was the sole passenger to detrain at La Plata; I thought this an odd, but perhaps good, omen: I liked the idea I was going to a place not frequented by others.

Until I had found a suitable place to rent I had decided to stay in a hotel, and I told the cabdriver to take me to the city's best hotel. As I later discovered, La Plata has only one hotel, but it was of a quality that suggested the best in any case. (La Plata, in fact, was a peculiarly singular city, I was to find: it had just one of almost everything, save churches and restaurants, of which it had only a few.)

The hotel was called the Excelsior, and the best room they had available was a large circular one on the top floor, in a turret. Its dramatic placement in the building made it almost inaccessible: I followed the bellhop from the elevator up a flight of stairs to the base of the turret. We ascended a wrought-iron spiral staircase to a little foyer with a grillwork floor. The bellhop unlocked the door and opened it into the room, moving aside so that I could enter first. The room was full of sunlight, and its rounded walls prevented the furniture from being arranged in a conventional pattern: the sofa and bed and desk and chairs were scattered almost haphazardly about.

A narrow wrought-iron balcony encircled the turret, and I stepped through the open French doors, which were slightly beveled to accommodate the curving walls. Directly below me, in front of the hotel, there lay a broad cobblestoned plaza, with a fountain at its center. Three bronze fishermen stood on a pile of rocks, casting lines of sparkling water into the air; flying fish rose up from the fountain's basin, exhaling spumes of water back at the fishermen. On the far side of the plaza, past a row of palm trees, a freshly raked red-gravel promenade surrounded the small harbor, which was full of small and colorful boats and a few ostentatious yachts. This promenade led in one direction to a flight of stone steps, at the top of which was a large, low building from whose open façade spilled an assortment of café tables and chairs. As I watched, a young man emerged from the restaurant and moved about the tables, unfurling red-and-white-striped umbrellas above them.

I thought I might have my lunch there.

At one end of the plaza stood a majestic building adorned with flags that suggested government, and facing it, at the opposite end, stood a correspondingly majestic building with an ornate glass-and-iron marquee that suggested entertainment. Assorted shops and some market stalls completed the square.

I walked a few steps along the balcony and a new and entirely different vista came into view: the stone houses of the town, which rose up from the plaza in a series of terraces. Each terrace was a subtly different shade of red, varying from terra cotta to maroon. Behind the last row of houses was a rather sheer cliff traversed by a funicular railway, the cars presently motionless, resting on the face of the cliff in vivid dots of red. There seemed to be a plateau at the top of the cliff, but I could not make out its character. Beyond that, though, higher up still, shimmering in the strong morning light, stood snow-capped mountains, and behind them, at the top of all this world, a sky of almost unnerving blue.

I had arrived with only one trunk, waiting until I was properly settled to have my belongings shipped. When I returned to the room I found a valet unpacking the trunk, which the bellboy had left at the foot of the bed. "Does the view agree with you?" he asked.

"Yes," I said, searching for a more enthusiastic affirmation. "It's very beautiful. Not at all what I expected."

"People are always surprised by Andorra," he said. "It is part of its charm." He unfolded my shirts, shook them crisply in the air, and then hung them in an armoire. Both mirrored doors of the armoire were flung open, so that there seemed to be several of him, and as many shirts. I stood and watched the spectacle of this. "Will you be having lunch with us?" he asked.

"I don't know," I said. "I thought I might try that place across the plaza. With the tables outside."

"The cantina," he said, "is delightful for lunch. Less formal than the hotel dining room. Although you might have a very nice lunch in the hotel garden. I could reserve you a table in the shade, if you would like."

"I think I'll venture out," I said.

"Of course." He took my shoes out of their cloth bags and lined them up across the bottom of the armoire. Then he closed the doors, latched my trunk, and said, "I'll bring this down to the cellar. Is there anything you need?"

"No," I said. "I'm very happily settled. Thank you." I gave him what seemed to me a large tip, which he accepted without comment.

"Enjoy your stay in Andorra," he said.

"Thank you," I said. "I intend to."

When the valet had departed I examined my interior world. The room had none of the lack of character one usually associates with a hotel. It was full not only of furniture but also of objects: Chinese porcelain bowls, alabaster eggs, a large leather-bound book on a wooden stand that I assumed was a Bible but was in fact a beautiful collection of sixteenth-century maps, with yesteryear's obsolete countries oddly elongated or squat, delicately colored in pastel hues. There were no cheap paintings bolted to the walls; in fact, the slight yet constant curve of the walls forbade paintings. They were decorated instead by a gilded cornice that encircled the ceiling, and a fresco painted in triptych, with a panel occurring in the few expanses of wall that the doors and windows allowed. Upon closer inspection I realized it was a depiction of Joan of Arc: a visionary Joan, a militant Joan, a Joan in flames.

I stood in the center of the room for a long time, allowing the glorious feeling of arrival to wash over me. Because we never know if we will get where we are going, it is always a relief to arrive there. I felt that I could live contentedly in this turret room of the Hotel Excelsior; perhaps I would stay there forever and allow my things to rot in storage, for after all, they were the things of my old life and I was starting anew.

Before I ventured out I took a bath in the large red granite tub in the bathroom, which had one window high up the wall, a window through which sunlight poured down into the bathwater, onto my body. I washed away the dust and grime of the past and I felt anointed, and welcomed; I felt that tragedy can be transcended, forgotten, annulled.

For the first time in a very long while, I felt calm.

CHAPTER TWO

※

BY THE TIME I EMERGED FROM THE HOTEL ONTO THE PLAZA the day had grown so warm that I found myself turning around to face the mountains, half expecting to discover them melting, for it was impossible to believe that the luxuriant heat that surrounded me didn't extend as far as the eye could see.

I circumnavigated the plaza's perimeter, noting the variety of shops, which seemed to be a perfect combination of the practical and the decadent: cobblers and stationers were the immediate neighbors of furriers and jewelers. I decided to visit the stationers. The front part of the store exhibited the expected paraphernalia, and a hall led to a room in back which contained fine paper from around the world. These papers were draped over wooden rods that skirted the room at various levels: one sheet of each, on display, like paintings. In the center of this room a glass case displayed an assortment of journals of varying sizes, bound by a variety of materials. It was not until I saw these journals that I realized that I wanted to write a book to record my new life. I wanted to put down, hour by hour, day by day, in some artful way, what I encountered, what had meaning to me, what I said and what was said to me, how I felt, and what I saw, so that if this new life failed, I would have a record, something left: a souvenir.

The books were all beautiful: bound in various leathers and fabrics, but one in particular drew my attention. It was a tall volume, almost twice as tall as it was wide, and its boards were covered with an exotically patterned fabric, in shades of rust and indigo. At my request a young man extracted this book from the case and explained to me that it had been created in Florence, from Japanese paper and Balinese fabric. I liked the fact that materials from the East had converged so beautifully in the West; it seemed to me to be a book of the world, and I bought it. From a case in the front of the store I selected and purchased a fountain pen made from some amber resin, which a clerk carefully filled with thick black squid ink, and I carried my two purchases out onto the plaza with a feeling of euphoria and expectation.

I completed my inspection of the plaza and walked along the promenade, which was bordered on one side with palm trees and the other by a low stone seawall against which the green water of the harbor listlessly insinuated itself. The red-and-white umbrellas of the cantina had all been hoisted—

It occurs to me as I write this that I may be overdescribing everything, relying too heavily on colors, and that the scene may appear garish and smudged. These descriptions may seem forced, but they are not, for Andorra was a place that forced me to describe it to myself as I experienced it. It was impossible to walk along that gravel path by the sea and not think *palm frond shadow*, for not only the path but I, my skin, was laced with it, a sort of breathing, shimmering tattoo. Colors had a boldness: nothing was pale; the sun seemed not to stun but to energize surfaces. Even objects had a heightened clarity, and if I am paying too much attention to the way things looked, it is only because in those first hours I felt myself in the world as never before. The world was vivid, all about me, as alive as I, and I felt myself, as if woken from a coma, alive in it.

The umbrella-shrouded tables outside the restaurant were all occupied, so I ambled through them and stood at the entrance. The interior was dark and comparatively empty. A long, deserted bar stretched across the back wall of the room, with tables scattered throughout the middle and placed evenly along the walls, one below each window. As no one appeared to seat me, I assumed a small table adjacent to a window that looked out onto an alley, on the other side of which was a tall stone wall almost completely covered with ivy.

The luncheon menu was not extensive; I ordered the table d'hôte and a pichet of native rosé wine. When the waiter brought my wine he also brought me a copy of the local English-language newspaper: *The La Plata Herald.* Apparently I had appeared to him in need of entertainment. A disturbing story on the first page related how a young man's body had been found, apparently murdered, in the harbor that morning. Citizens were urged to take caution when walking alone at night. Another front-page story reported that the director of the opera had either been fired or resigned after a dispute regarding a controversial staging of *Nabucco.*

The large face of a dog suddenly appeared beside my newspaper and I looked up to see a tall blond woman escorted by this animal. The dog sat beside my chair and stared at me. It was the largest dog I had ever seen — its face was level with my own.

"I'm sorry," said the woman, tugging, to no avail, on the animal's lead. "Dino's rather a creature of habit. This is usually our table."

"Oh, pardon me," I said. "I'll move."

"No, no," the woman said. "Don't think of it." She looked around the room, and though there were many empty tables, none of them seemed right for her. "But perhaps we could join you?" she asked. "If you wouldn't mind. Otherwise I'll have to keep tugging Dino out of your face."

"That would be fine," I said. "But I really have no problem with changing tables."

"Oh," the woman said. "I'm sorry. You don't want company."

"No," I said. "It's not that at all."

"Good," she said, and smiled at me. "Down," she said to Dino, who sighed and very slowly lowered his body to the floor. I folded the newspaper and stood up as the woman sat opposite me. "Oops," she said, reaching beneath her, "what's this?" She held out my package from the stationers, which the clerk had wrapped in gold paper and tied with a scarlet ribbon. "What a lovely package!"

I took it from her and laid it on the windowsill. The woman sat down, and as I did, she reached out her hand and said, "My name is Ricky Dent. It's very nice of you to share your table."

I shook her hand and told her my name. "It's you who are sharing your table," I said, resuming my seat.

"Well, you got here first," she said. "What do they say: Possession is the better half of ownership?"

"Nine-tenths," I said.

"Well, that's certainly the better half." She laughed. She had an easy friendly laugh, and a slight awkwardness about her I found endearing. She had an odd angular face that could appear either plain or attractive, depending on her expression and the angle from which it was regarded.

"So you come here often for lunch?"

"Every day," she said. "Every weekday, at least. Unless it's raining, which of course it never is. Dino and I make a walk out of it. I don't believe I've seen you in here before."

"I've just arrived in Andorra this morning."

"Have you? From where? For how long?"

"Most immediately from Paris. And the United States before that. I'm in the process of moving to Andorra. I plan to live here."

"Good for you," she said, as if I were a child who had done something not very difficult well.

"I take it you live here?"

"I do," she said. "Or have been, and seem to go on doing. For quite a while now. My husband and I retired here from Australia."

"You seem awfully young to be retired," I said.

"We got lucky," she said, "and made a big pot of money—Ricky did; my husband's also called Ricky—and decided to chuck it all and come here."

"And are you happy here?" I asked.

Before she could answer the waiter appeared. Mrs. Dent told him, "As usual." She looked down at her empty hands for a moment and then looked up at me. "Actually," she said, "I'm not very happy at the moment."

"I'm sorry," I said. "It was a rude question."

She gave a quick, sad smile and shrugged. "Who's the lovely package for?" she asked.

"For myself," I said.

"And what does a man like you buy himself?"

"I bought a journal. I thought I'd keep a record of my—"

"Of your new life?" she suggested.

"Yes. That's what it seems like to me."

"It seemed that way to me, too, when I arrived. How quickly new lives become old lives! I kept a diary when I was a girl. Filled it with nonsense. What will you write in yours?"

"Oh," I said, "I don't really know. It was a whimsical purchase. I thought I'd keep a record of my days. I want to try to live my life more deliberately, more consciously. I thought keeping a journal might help."

"If you spend all your time recording your life, you'll have no time to live it," she said.

"I hope it won't come to that."

Our food arrived: a broiled trout for me and a chicken-and-avocado salad for Mrs. Dent. "Where are you staying?" she asked, as we began eating.

"At the Excelsior," I said.

"How posh," she said.

"Yes," I said. "It's quite beautiful. I'm thinking about staying there awhile, although I intend to find a place of my own before too long."

"It isn't easy to find places. Especially at this time of year." She speared a piece of chicken with her fork and held it down to the dog, who devoured it in a single bite. "For how long do you want a place?"

"Forever," I said.

"That's a very long time," she said.

"Well, perhaps not forever. But I want to settle down here. I don't want to move again."

"What brought you to Andorra?" Mrs. Dent asked. Dino had sat up and was patiently awaiting his next bite of lunch. I didn't answer the question, and Mrs. Dent looked over at me. She narrowed her eyes in an attempt to read my expression, and laid down her fork. "I'm sorry. Now it's I who's asking unfortunate questions. Of course it's none of my business what brought you to Andorra. Say the wind brought you, or fate, or something silly like that, but have an answer ready, for people are bound to ask you. I can guarantee you that."

"I think it was fate," I said.

"I have no doubt," she said. "It brought us all." We ate for quite a while in silence, and then Mrs. Dent said, "Ricky used to come down and have lunch with me every day, but now he thinks it's too much of a bother. That's what I mean about new lives getting old. Why aren't you eating at the hotel?"

"I was anxious to explore the town."

"I could show you around a bit when we're done eating, if you'd like." She made this offer with little enthusiasm, as if anticipating a rejection.

I did not want to take advantage of Mrs. Dent's offer. She seemed charming, but something about her did not seem quite safe, and until I understood the social terrain, I thought it might be a mistake to extend myself any further in her direction. Sometimes it is not in one's best interest to make friends too quickly—one makes the wrong friends. "I'm feeling rather tired after my journey," I said. "I think I'd benefit from a siesta."

"Of course," she said. She forked the last bit of meat into Dino's waiting mouth. "But I'm not so easily deterred. Would you come up to dinner some evening? I'd love for you to meet my husband. Ricky doesn't—Most of the men we know are rather aged and stuffy. And I'm so sure he'd like you. You aren't stuffy, are you?"

"Not deliberately," I said.

"You're not at all," she said, reaching out and touching my hand. "You're very sweet, and charming, and it was my great good fortune to discover you before anyone else did." She stood up. "Come, my pet," she said to Dino, who stood beside her. "I'll give you a day or two to settle in, and then leave you a proper invitation for dinner. And perhaps we can lunch together again. I'd like that. I've enjoyed it so very much." She extended her hand.

I stood up and shook it. "So have I," I said. "Thank you for the pleasure."

She smiled at me, and then patted Dino's flank. "You're very welcome," she said.

We made our goodbyes and I waited until she went through the door before I sat down. The waiter came and cleared away our dishes and then brought me my tart. After the intrusion of Mrs. Dent I enjoyed being alone, and to prolong the meal I ordered another glass of wine. The room had emptied and the waiters loitered at the bar. I could see through the windows that the tables out front had been mostly vacated, as had the plaza. It was time for a siesta; I could feel the town withdrawing itself behind closed doors, shutters, between sheets.

I lifted my golden package from the windowsill and held it for a moment in my hands, as if I did not know and was trying to discern its content. And then I tugged on the scarlet ribbon and watched it transform itself from a blossom into a narrow piece of cloth. The paper fell to the floor in a rustling whoosh of gold, and I touched the fabric covers, traced their swirling pattern with my finger. And then I opened the book to the first impossibly blank beautiful page, withdrew my new fountain pen from my jacket pocket, uncapped it, and wrote, in ink that glistened and seemed as thick and permeable as blood: *Many years ago I read a book . . .*

CHAPTER THREE

I HAD LOOKED FORWARD TO RESUMING MY EXPLORATION OF THE town in the afternoon, but after telling Mrs. Dent I intended to take a siesta, I found myself heading straight back to the hotel to do exactly that. I changed my plans for two reasons — no, three: I did not want to allow an untruth to mar the first day of my new life; I was a little afraid that had I continued my wanderings I may have embarrassingly encountered Ricky Dent and Dino; and I was tired.

And I had plenty of time to explore La Plata: in the beginning, you are never rushed.

The windows and French doors of my hotel room were all open and a fresh sea breeze cooled the room. I took off my clothes, and as I approached the bed I noticed its feet were fitted with small bronze wheels; with a slight push I was able to move it across the floor. A skein of sunlight fell through the balcony doors and I moved the bed into the sun's warm wake, and then hoisted myself up onto the high, soft feather mattress, so that the sun fell on me. I lay for a while looking down at the harbor, which sent frantic signals of refracted light back up into the sky.

When I awoke the sun had fallen, the light had changed, and the breeze coming through the door was almost chilly. For a moment I was disoriented and lost, and then my whereabouts and recent events filtered slowly up into my consciousness: the overnight train ride from Paris, the hotel, the journal, the lunch with Mrs. Dent . . .

I looked down at my body, which had been burned a bit by the sun flooding my bed: a prickly redness on my stomach and legs. When I touched the red skin it blushed white, and when I removed my finger it returned red. My body had once been fine: lithe and strong and well shaped, but now it looked none of those things; I had let it slip, I had failed it, ignored it. Forgotten it almost.

I stepped out of bed onto the stone floor and stood with my feet apart and my arms raised as high as I could reach them above my head, my fingers extended and pointing to the ceiling of the turret, and then I rose up on my toes and stood like that, stretched, for a count of ten. I repeated this exercise several times and then did some bending and stretching movements, followed by a number of push-ups and sit-ups. When I was through with these calisthenics my body felt sore and I was breathless, yet I felt not tired but invigorated. I would do this every day, I vowed, every day without fail, and my body would return to its old, beautiful self.

There was a bottle of mineral water on the bedside table (which was no longer beside the bed): an emerald-green bottle. I opened it and poured some water, which hissed and fizzed, into a tumbler. The water had a swampy taste and odor, but it slaked my thirst and I poured a second glass. As I drank I noticed my journal, which I had left on a strange piece of furniture in an alcove just inside the door. I assumed it was a prie-dieu: it had a low velvet-covered surface near to the floor and at the top of an intricately carved wood column a little stand, inlaid with mother-of-pearl, with a ledge to support a book. My journal was a bit too tall for the stand, but otherwise looked very handsome perched there: the batiked fabric of its cover matched the faded velvet of the hassock. I debated writing about my lunch with Mrs. Dent in its pages, and then decided she was right: I had to do as much living of life as recording of it, so I put on my clothes and went out to continue my exploration of the town.

Upon my return to the hotel that evening, I was informed by the concierge that there were two seatings for dinner, as on a ship: the first at seven o'clock and the second at nine o'clock. I asked him to reserve me a table at the earlier time. I would normally have chosen the latter, as earlier seatings are notoriously the province of children and the elderly, but it had been a long day and I was tired, despite — or perhaps because of — my nap; a taste of sleep in the afternoon often makes me crave my bed in the evening.

I had caught a glimpse of the dining room as I passed through the lobby. It was a large, formal, high-ceilinged room with windows facing both the street and the small private garden directly behind the hotel; the walls were frescoed and the ceiling gilded. It looked quite beautiful as I entered it a little after seven o'clock: candles and flowers adorned each table, and three chandeliers diffused a dim light which warmed the golden ceiling and refracted itself in the crystals which encrusted them. I was shown to a small table against the far wall that had only one chair and obviously was intended for a solo diner, and I was relieved to be seated there, for I realized I was a little panicked lest I should be descended upon again, à la Ricky Dent. Although, as I thought about it, I realized I had enjoyed my lunch with Mrs. Dent: she was a curious person, both off-putting and engaging, frank and cryptic. I realized I would not mind seeing her again, and hoped that she might reappear soon, as she had promised, with an invitation to dinner.

I have dined alone often enough so that I should be relaxed about it, but I rarely am. I am too aware of being alone; and I feel that since I have no one at whom to direct my attention, my fellow diners all think I am observing them, eavesdropping, and generally being rude. And sometimes they look at me with pity, and smile, which I cannot stand. I often bring a book to divert my attention, and I had stopped in the hotel library on my way down to dinner. After quickly perusing its shelves (which were stocked with leather-bound classics of English, French, Russian, and ancient Greek literature), I had selected a volume of Trollope, which I had brought with me to the table, yet I left this volume unopened beside my plate. I know something of etiquette, but there seem to be no firm rules regarding reading when dining alone in restaurants: I think it depends upon the establishment and the company in which one is dining. I sensed that reading in the dining room of the Hotel Excelsior would be incongruous with the tone of the room, so I gave my attention to my meal, which was excellent (consommé, roasted pheasant, a salad of bitter greens, some local sheep's cheese, pear tart; a half bottle of Médoc), and between courses studied the frescoes, the view of the plaza fading in the late-evening light, and, surreptitiously, my fellow diners.

After dinner the hotel provided a number of distractions: there was a lounge which served cocktails, a billiard and smoking room, a lounge which didn't serve cocktails, and the library. As my choice of Trollope had been made in haste, I decided to return it and see if I couldn't find something else to bring with me to bed.

The library was a cramped, oddly shaped room—its shape reminded me of a picture-puzzle piece—whose walls were entirely covered with shelves of books, beautiful mahogany shelves that formed a series of intimate alcoves around the room. A small light was affixed to the top of each case, which one could illuminate, I discovered, by pressing an antique-looking switch built into the shelf at eye level. The resulting light stayed on for a few minutes, and then extinguished itself. I had loitered in a secluded bay devoted to modern British literature for more than three intervals of light, when I discovered a copy of *Crewe Train* by Rose Macaulay, the very book that had prompted me to move to Andorra. I had read it very long ago. If I read it again now, what would I think? Should I let my memory of it alone? Sometimes it is dangerous to revisit a loved book, especially after a great change in one's life: the book no longer seems perfect; one swears it has been altered or edited, when in fact it is, of course, oneself who has been revised. I slipped the book from the shelf and held it as the light went off again, and for once I took a darkening to be an affirmative signal: Yes, take the book. Go to bed.

As I withdrew from my alcove, I noticed that I was sharing the library. There was one round table at the center of the room, on which neatly arranged newspapers and periodicals encircled a huge ceramic vase of hydrangeas, and at this table sat an elderly lady, dressed simply and elegantly in black. Her blue-white hair was the exact color of the hydrangeas. She had pearls in her ears and diamonds about her neck. "Good evening," she said to me, and I realized that she had been sitting there, waiting for me to emerge.

"Good evening," I said.

"Did you find something you like?"

"Yes," I said. I held out *Crewe Train.*

She made a pretense of squinting and said, "My eyes aren't what they were."

"Oh," I said. "It's *Crewe Train.* By Rose Macaulay."

"Why of course," she said. "How appropriate."

"I read it once a long time ago," I said, "and I remember it being about Andorra. So now that I'm here, I thought I'd take another look."

"Rose got it all wrong," the woman said. "She never came to Andorra—she went everywhere else, or liked to think she did, but never Andorra. Her portrait of our country is very inaccurate."

"Did you know her?" I asked.

"Quite well," the woman said. "She always scared me, just a bit. Made me feel a silly fool." She held out her hand and said, "I am Lucille Reinhardt."

I shook her hand, which, being all loose skin and bones, felt spookily unlike a hand, and told her my name.

"Will you sit with me a moment?" she asked. "Or are you so eager to be off to bed with Rose?"

I sat down.

"I'm always intrigued when someone ventures into the library," she said. "I keep my eyes, such as they are, peeled. It happens less often than you would think. Do you like books?"

"Yes," I said. "Very much. I once owned a bookstore."

"Did you?" she said. "What a noble thing to do. My father was a publisher. Lord Houck, of Houck & Dean. It's through him that I met Rose Macaulay. My father adored books. Most of these are his." She nodded toward the shelves.

"Are they?" I said. "It's a wonderful library."

"It's from my family home, in Barsetshire. When my parents both died, and we closed the house, I had the library shipped here. Shelves and all. Even this table," she said, and touched, with her shriveled hand, the smooth wood. "It cost a fortune, but it was worth every penny."

"You gave the books to the hotel?" I asked.

"In a manner of speaking," she said. "The hotel was once mine. I married Hervé Reinhardt, the owner of the Hotel Excelsior, in 1922. And when he died, God rest his soul, in 1943, I sold the hotel. I sold it for next to nothing, but with the condition that I could live in it—in a suite, mind you—and have my meals in it for the remainder of my days. Those who bought it thought it a very good deal, but I'm ninety-four years old now and have no intention of dying. Living's easy when it's free. I've done very well for myself. So the hotel no longer belongs to me, although the books still do. Perhaps that is why I take such delight when someone comes in here, and looks at them. Really looks at them—not glances. I was watching you. And you say you owned a bookstore?"

"Yes," I said, "once I did. With my wife."

"Your wife? Is she traveling with you?"

I was flustered, for I had not intended to mention my wife, or anything about my old life, ever again. "No," I said. "She has pre-deceased me."

"I'm so sorry, but what an odd way of saying it," Mrs. Reinhardt said.

I was silent.

"Bookstores aren't a thing to own," she said. "Hotels do nicely, believe me. But I'm keeping you from your book. I only wanted to say good evening to you, and welcome. How long are staying with us?"

"I'm planning to live in La Plata. I'll stay at the hotel until I find a place."

"What sort of place do you need?"

I shrugged. "I don't know. I've just begun to look around."

"I ask because I know of a place that may be available. My friend Mrs. Quay is looking to let her brother-in-law's small house, which is up on the third terrace. He's had to go off somewhere—she told me where, the Argentine or Ceylon or some such place, but I've forgotten. And she doesn't want just anybody, if you know what I mean, and she's loath to advertise, and that's why she was telling me about it, because she thought someone appropriate might turn up at the hotel. I've never seen it, but if it's the Quays', it's nice, I can guarantee you that. He's a confirmed bachelor, Mr. Quay, a fine man with good taste, so I imagine his house is livable."

"Is it difficult to find places?" I asked.

"It's an awful thing," she said. "That's why I'm still in the hotel, why I made my bargain. So I'd never have to look, or worry. You see, people don't like to leave Andorra, and there are always new people coming, people like you, and others not as nice. It's an awful thing."

"Well then, Mr. Quay's home seems like an opportunity. I'd be most grateful if you spoke to your friend on my behalf."

"I'll send her word in the morning. I doubt she's found anyone yet, because she's awfully discerning. He's left all his things behind, you see, and she doesn't want just anyone living with them. I assume you're looking for a furnished place."

"I have some things in storage, but I'm in no hurry to see them again, so that would be perfect," I said.

"I knew I followed you in here for a reason," Mrs. Reinhardt said. "At my age, most things happen for a reason. I suppose they do at any age, but it is all much more obvious now. I'll write Mrs. Quay in the morning. I'm sure it will all work out perfectly."

"You're very kind," I said.

"How nice of you to think that," she said. "Kindness is always mostly perceived, I've found. What I mean to say is that kind people most appreciate kindness. Which is to say, you are kind."

"Thank you," I said.

"Would you do me a kindness?" she asked. "If I were so bold as to ask you one?"

"Of course," I said. "I would be delighted."

"It would be very kind of you to read me a page or two from Miss Macaulay. My eyes don't see well enough to read anymore, and the lass from the Girl Guides who reads to me on Wednesdays has a rather uninflected voice. And that's being kind of me."

"I don't think I'm an awfully good reader," I said.

"I'm sure you're better than my Girl Guide, God bless her," said Mrs. Reinhardt.

"Should I read the beginning?" I asked, picking up the book.

"Yes," she said. "Start at the beginning. Which isn't to imply that I expect you to read any more than the beginning."

CHAPTER FOUR

When I woke at dawn, it was raining hard, blowing through the open balcony doors onto the floor and the bed. I closed the doors and mopped the floor with a towel and then stood and watched the rain pelt the glass. It ran in rivulets across the empty plaza; the basin of the fountain had overflowed and created a little lake in the plaza's center. I drew the drapes across the doors and fell back asleep.

My breakfast was brought to me by the same valet who had unpacked my bags the day before. He stood in the middle of the room, holding a silver tray, and said, "Would you like it in bed, sir, or on the table?"

"The table," I said.

"Would you like me to open the drapes?"

"No thank you."

"Very well. Is there anything else I could get you?"

"No," I said. "Thank you."

I remained in my room all morning, writing in my journal and reading *Crewe Train*. I had read the first chapter of *Crewe Train* to Mrs. Reinhardt, and the Andorra described in its pages was very unlike the country in which I found myself. I mentioned this fact to Mrs. Reinhardt, who reassured me that the author had never been to Andorra and was known for her vivid imagination and propensity to take liberties with geography.

It was still raining at midday, a slow patient rain, although the sky had brightened. I stood for a long while looking down at the world and saw Mrs. Dent and her large dog hastening across the plaza, both of them wearing bright yellow slickers, no doubt headed toward the cantina for lunch. I had considered having my own lunch there, but decided to have it brought up to my room, and when it arrived there was an envelope on the tray, addressed to me at the hotel.

The thick sheet of paper I extracted from the envelope had the word QUAYSIDE discreetly engraved at its top. The date had been written beneath that in a large, elegant hand; there was no salutation, just a sort of flourish across the top of the page and the following message:

Mrs. Reinhardt was good enough to send me word this morning that you are seeking lodgings in our beautiful city. I believe she mentioned to you the availability of my brother-in-law's house. It is a small house, though charming, on the third terrace — high but not too high — with nice rooms and a splendid view. There is, alas, no garden. I am willing to rent it (to the right person, of course) at a very reasonable rate for a period of one year. If you are interested, why don't you come to tea today so that we could meet one another and discuss this further? I assume that you are eager to be settled. I should be happy to show you the house at that time, or later, as you so wish. Come even if you are not interested — Mrs. Reinhardt writes that you are delightful (and Mrs. Reinhardt is never wrong!) and so we should like to make your acquaintance. We have tea at 4:30. Anyone can give you directions to Quayside, which is a short walk from the hotel, past the cantina and out the peninsula road.

Isn't this rain awful? The rumor is that you brought it with you, but if you come to tea all will be forgiven.

It was signed Sophonsobia Doyle Quay (Mrs.).

I considered this letter as I ate my lunch. Its lack of greeting was odd, and as I reread it I found that it left me in the uncomfortable position of imbibing tea at Quayside or appearing rude; no option for refusing the invitation was given. I supposed I could pretend the letter never reached me, but that seemed disingenuous, and potentially compromising. And the hurry of it all seemed odd to me: Mrs. Reinhardt must have been up at dawn, and messengers must have shuttled back and forth between the hotel and Quayside throughout the rainy morning.

I set out from the hotel into the cool and moist afternoon. The rain had stopped and the sun fell through the disintegrating clouds in long, slanted streams; the plaza steamed; the air smelt of clean earth and wet lilacs. I stopped into the cantina, which appeared deserted, for directions to Quayside and some Dutch courage. It was deserted, save for Mrs. Dent and Dino, who occupied the table we had shared the day before. Mrs. Dent appeared to be working a crossword puzzle; Dino was asleep at her feet. She looked up as I approached the bar, behind which the bartender was toweling glasses dry.

"Funny meeting you here," she said, tapping her pencil against her rather large teeth.

"Yes," I said.

"I thought you might come to lunch."

"I had lunch in my hotel room," I said. "I didn't much feel like venturing out."

"I know," she said. "The weather's rotten. I'm waiting for the rain to stop before I push off home."

"It has stopped," I said.

"Has it?" she asked. She gazed out into the alley, where obviously no rain was falling, and said, "It's hard to tell from in here." She looked over at me, her head to one side, and said, "Can I stand you a drink? Or would you like to share a pot of tea? It's a nice day for tea, isn't it?"

"I'm sorry, but I've just stopped in for directions."

"Oh," she said, "where are you off to?"

I looked at her. I still didn't trust Mrs. Dent, so I didn't want to tell her I was on my way to visit the Quays at Quayside. I didn't answer.

"Forgive me," she said. "It's no business of mine where you're off to." She returned her attention, rather exaggeratedly, to her puzzle.

The bartender, who had obviously heard our interchange, regarded me. I didn't know what to do. If I asked him for directions in a normal tone of voice, Mrs. Dent was sure to hear, and it would be awkward to whisper. I was standing in the center of the room, my fists thrust into the pockets of my raincoat. I could think of nothing to do except turn around and walk back into the street, which I did, certain that my sheepish exit was observed by both the bartender and Mrs. Dent. I stood for a moment at the top of the steps leading up from the plaza. I assumed the peninsula road lay directly behind the cantina, which meant I would have to proceed up the alley past Mrs. Dent's window. I was trying to figure out if I could walk around the other side of the building when the door opened and Mrs. Dent emerged, sans Dino. "Hello," she said.

I said hello.

"That was bloody awkward, wasn't it?" She nodded toward the cantina's interior. "I didn't want you to leave with that . . . awkwardness between us. I'd be happy to give you directions, if you'd like. You're off to Quayside, I believe?"

"Yes," I said. "How did you know?"

"You've been rather the talk of the town this morning," she said. "You'd be surprised what I know about you."

I remembered mentioning my wife to Mrs. Reinhardt. "What else do you know?" I asked.

"I know you read Rosamond Lehmann aloud to Mrs. Reinhardt in the hotel library last night."

"Actually, it was Rose Macaulay. And I'll be more careful from now on. I didn't know I was under constant surveillance."

"What is it that you want to hide?" asked Mrs. Dent.

"Everything," I said.

"You might have an easier time of it if you narrowed it down a bit. Hiding everything makes one rather a target."

"I'll keep that in mind," I said.

"Just a bit of friendly advice," she said, and smiled. She really had a very nice smile: a bit crooked, but totally genuine. "I would so like to be friends with you," she said, looking now at her feet. "But only if you would like that as well."

"I would," I said, "very much."

She looked back at me. "I'm so glad," she said. "You've no idea. I like you very much and I have so few friends." And then, as if this admission embarrassed her, she changed her tone and said, "So you're off to Quayside?"

"Yes," I said. "For tea. They have a lead about a house I might rent."

"Follow the alley up the hill onto the road. Turn left and follow the road out along the peninsula. You can't miss the Quay estate. It's about half a mile out on your right. The gates are festooned with rather ostentatious Qs." She drew a Q in the air with her finger. "Perhaps I'll see you for lunch tomorrow," she said.

"Perhaps," I said. "I'm not sure of my plans."

"Of course," she said, "nor am I of mine. Plans: I could do with some, I suppose. I better get back to Dino. Good luck with the Quays." She held out her hand, and I shook it, and then she returned inside the cantina and I made my way up the alley, waving to her through the window as I passed.

The peninsula road was a straight narrow deserted lane that seemed to traverse the highest point of the peninsula, although the large trees planted at regular intervals along both its sides prevented one from seeing, or even sensing, the water. Since I had denied myself a drink, I arrived at the massive gates of Quayside earlier and in a less relaxed state than I had intended. The entrance to Quayside was, as Mrs. Dent had described, hard to miss: a tall stone wall fronted the road, interrupted only by a huge elaborate iron gate, the scrollwork of which featured two huge Qs surrounded by an exhalation of smaller ones. The gate was closed, but through it I could see a neat gravel drive bordered by a manicured privet. The drive curved down and out of sight. I was about a quarter of an hour early, and I decided to wait for the appointed time before trying to enter the gates, as I had the feeling visitors at Quayside were expected to be punctual. A short way past the gate a stone bench was placed in the shade of a tree. I unfolded my handkerchief and spread it out on the seat to protect my pants from damp and lichen, and sat down. As I waited, the sky succeeded in clearing itself. At exactly half past four I returned to the gate, and opened it wide enough to allow my entrance. I walked down the immaculately raked gravel drive and around a curve, where the privet ceased, the vista opened, and I could see a house poised on the cliff above the sea.

It was not as grand a house as the gates and the drive suggested. I had expected something huge and foolish, and this house was neither: it had the appearance of a château, and I was struck by its beauty and pleasing proportions. It appeared from this vantage point about as tall as it was wide, with classical façades of ivy-covered gray stone. A copper mansard roof, patinaed a lovely soft green, was washed clean by the rain and shone in the newly emerged sun. A maid moved from room to room on an upper floor, opening wide the casement windows, pushing the panes of glass out into the sunlit air, like wings. The house was square, with the exception of a tall peaked tower, also copper-clad, at the corner nearest to the sea. A large porte cochere extended out from the front of the house over the drive. The lawn, which sloped down toward the house in

a wide expanse, was studded with large islands of magenta rhodo-
dendrons and cerulean hydrangeas.

After admiring the house for a moment, I continued down the
drive, under the porte cochere, up two or three stone steps, and
made use of the Q-shaped knocker that hung from the middle of
the large wooden door.

It was opened immediately by a woman wearing a linen dress of
the palest lilac. She seemed to be as tall as I, and I had the unusual
experience of looking directly into, rather than down at, her face.
She had an odd face: almost pretty, with fine features and very
large gray-green eyes, but her face, like the rest of her, was a little
too large, somehow, and her expression seemed infused with sadness and toil, despite her welcoming smile. She appeared to be a
woman who always had something troubling on her mind, yet took
great pains to hide it, and for this reason, it was hard to discern her
age. She held out her hand to me and said, "I am Miss Quay. You
must be Mr. Fox. We're so happy that you've come. You'll have to
forgive me answering the door. We've had a bit of a flood in the
basement and our butler is down there moving things about."

"Perhaps it's an inconvenient time for me to arrive," I said, shaking her hand.

"Oh no," she said, standing aside so that I could enter the hall.
"We are undaunted by these occurrences." The hall was a large
room with a slate floor and a wooden staircase going up and around
its walls, first along one and then along another, rising up in this
manner to the top of the house.

"Since the sun returned we're having tea on the loggia, though there's a bit of a breeze. Mother's awaiting us. Will you follow me?"

She walked across the hall and opened a paneled wooden door by sliding it into the wall, and I followed her into a large salon with many gilt-legged sofas and chairs, which all appeared to be spread as far apart from one another as possible. It took us a moment to traverse the expanse of this room; Miss Quay walked before me and once or twice turned around to check my progress, as if I might get lost or grow fatigued, each time offering me her sad smile. At the far end of this room, which we finally achieved, was a series of Palladian glass doors, one of which, being already opened, we passed through. The loggia, full of plants and Victorian wicker furniture, was as cozy as the salon was grand. Miss Quay indicated with a large hand the seat she wished me to assume, and then sat down across from me. A silver tea set gleamed on the low rattan table between us.

"I don't know where Mother's gone off to," she said. "She may be checking her kayak. The tide was extraordinarily high this morning, and she was afraid it might be carried out to sea. It's happened twice before."

"Your mother kayaks?" I asked.

"Yes," said Miss Quay. "She's very much an outdoorswoman. She rode every day until she broke her hip, but now she prefers kayaking. And archery." She indicated a target set on the lawn near the cliff's edge. This lawn was bisected by a path of crushed white shells, and as we spoke, a woman's body rose above the precipice. She seemed tall from a distance, and grew taller the nearer she came. She held a cane but did not seem to use it. She waved it, a bit wildly above her head, and called, "Hallo! Hallo! Greetings!"

"That's Mother," said Miss Quay.

I stood up as Mrs. Quay approached the loggia. "Greetings," she said once more. "I see you have met my daughter. I am Mrs. Quay. Welcome to Andorra and, more particularly, to Quayside." She sat upon a small love seat between her daughter and me. "My kayak is fine," she announced. "Bitsy's beach toys are no longer with us, but the tide knew well enough to leave my kayak alone." She turned to me. "And it's a good thing, too," she said. "For it's an awful bother to get a new one. Do you know where I get my kayaks?"

"No," I said.

"From Lapland," she said. "It is the only place where they still know how to make kayaks. Mine are made especially for me by an Arctic fisherwoman, and I would be very sorry to lose it."

"I see," I said.

"Shall I pour the tea, Mother?" asked Miss Quay. "Assam or oolong, Mr. Fox?"

"Oolong," I said.

The pouring of tea, which Miss Quay did very expertly, consumed our attention for a minute or two. Mrs. Quay offered me a plate of delicate-looking sandwiches. "Cucumber, I'm afraid," she said. "We are very conventional when it comes to tea. If you join us for another meal, I assure you you will dine more interestingly."

"These look delicious," I said, taking one.

"They are," said Mrs. Quay. "And nothing tastes better with tea. I understand that you have only recently arrived in Andorra?"

"Yes," I said, "I began my expatriate life yesterday."

"That is a life you will have to begin elsewhere," Mrs. Quay said, setting the plate of sandwiches back on the tea tray. "There are no expatriates in Andorra."

"Really?" I said. "It was my impression that there were many."

"No, we are patriots, one and all," said Mrs. Quay. "Anyone living in Andorra is considered a citizen. It's part of our constitution. You are correct—a majority of the population is not indigenous, but they are in no way discriminated against or considered outsiders. There is no outside in Andorran society, in fact. It is one of the many advantages of living in so small a country. Do you know anything about the history of your new country?"

"To be perfectly honest," I said, "I don't. And I'm rather ashamed. I've never read very much about Andorra in terms of the history of the world. Or Europe, for that matter."

"We are a part of Europe only in the most strictly geographical sense," said Mrs. Quay.

"Mother," said Miss Quay, "you're sounding very lectoral."

"I'm sorry," said Mrs. Quay. "I'm sure you're right, Jean. Forgive me, Mr. Fox."

"Not at all," I said. "I would be gratified to learn something of Andorra's history."

Mrs. Quay sipped her tea, and considered. "Well," she began, "to a certain extent you're correct: we have not much history of strife or war or hardship, and that is usually the history that gets recorded and talked about. Andorra was originally settled by the Romans. The harbor was much larger and deeper then—it has filled with silt over the centuries—and was used as a sort of way station in transporting goods between the East and the West. The wall in the Hotel Excelsior garden is Roman, as are many of the roads in the old town. Caterina de' Medici visited Andorra and loved it so much she tried to establish a court here under Henry II; the castle, which was supposedly one of the loveliest in Europe, was totally ransacked in the eighteenth century. But she developed a plan for our city that has been followed to this day and is responsible for the uniform appearance of all the buildings. She decreed that all stone must come from the native quarries; it is a type of red granite found nowhere else in the world. It is what gives the town its singular appearance, for as it ages, the color deepens. The city has expanded up the hill in terraces, and each terrace is a slightly different, but complementary, shade.

"Politically, there is not much to speak of. A degenerate monarchy gave way to a small elected governing body in 1780; we adapted de Mirabeau's model constitution for a new-world democracy, and it has never needed alteration or amendment. The only subsequent unrest occurred in the 1960s. The country is, as you have no doubt noticed, divided topographically into the lower and upper berths, as it were: the lower comprising the harbor and the peninsula, and of course La Plata; the upper, reachable only by funicular and cog railway, is comprised of the Vega and the mountains. The country's wealth, which is considerable, was unequally divided between these two parts—the villages of the Vega, which are populated mainly by hardworking agrarians, did not have the health and educational facilities of the city. They rebelled, in a manner of speaking—it was very tame: placards, marches, a few threats—and the injustice was quickly realized and attended to. My late husband, Reginald Quay, was Secretary of Domestic Affairs at that time and was the creator of the Upland Initiative. Have you heard of the Initiative?"

"No," I said.

"It was one of the most successful economic redistribution and revitalization programs of its time. It was praised by your President Johnson. Of course, one of the advantages of a country the size of Andorra is that such initiatives are possible; change can happen. And thanks to my husband, it did."

"You must be very proud of him," I said.

"I am," said Mrs. Quay. "He was a compassionate, forward-thinking man."

"That was a very pretty speech, Mother," said Miss Quay. "More tea, Mr. Fox?"

"Please," I said, and handed her my cup.

"Well, now you know a little of Andorra's past," said Mrs. Quay. "I don't think that's such a bad thing. It will help you to live in its present. But I understand you want a place to live, which brings you to us."

"Yes," I said. "Nice as it is, I can't stay at the Hotel Excelsior forever."

"Certainly not," said Mrs. Quay. "Their tariffs are outrageous. When the Reinhardts owned the hotel it did not exploit the public in the shameless way it does now. It rankles me to know you are its prisoner."

I had found the rates at the Excelsior very reasonable, but I refrained from sharing this with Mrs. Quay. "It would be nice to be more permanently settled," I said.

"Of course," she said. "Which brings us to Roddy's house. My brother-in-law Roderick is in Ceylon. The government there is being very difficult about the logging of our teak, and it will take some time to straighten it all out. He left abruptly a week ago. I couldn't help but think that your almost simultaneous arrival was in some way providential. I am a firm believer in providence."

"Mother, you believe in nothing tepidly," said Miss Quay.

"I suppose that is true. Would you care to see the house this evening, Mr. Fox? Or do you have other engagements?"

"This evening would be convenient for me," I said.

Miss Quay had stepped down onto the lawn. She stood on the shell path, looking out at the sea, where she made an imposing figure: her linen dress blown against her strong, tall body. I realized the prospect of being escorted solely by Mrs. Quay did not please me: I felt her lecture was not yet—would never be—completed. "Will you join us, Miss Quay?" I asked.

She turned to look at me, and for a moment the veil of turmoil seemed lifted from her face and I realized that she was very beautiful: tall and strong, with fine brown hair pulled back from her face and simply collected against the back of her head. "I don't think—" she began, but was interrupted by her mother, who banged her cane against the terra-cotta floor and said, "Nonsense. Why don't the two of you go alone? You need me for nothing. And I am a little tired from my trek down to the beach. Or, more precisely, from my trek back up."

CHAPTER FIVE

*M*ISS QUAY AND I MADE WHAT IS CONVENTIONALLY REFERRED
to as polite conversation as we walked along the peninsula road. As
we neared the harbor, I realized that I was apprehensive: I feared
we would encounter Mrs. Dent outside the cantina. I felt sure she
had retained her post by the alley window, awaiting my return, and
the prospect of her seeing me with Miss Quay troubled me. But
Miss Quay led me past the alley, explaining that the peninsula road
led more directly to the third terrace, and therefore to her uncle's
house. I immediately felt ashamed of my apprehension, and while
paying adequate attention to Miss Quay's undemanding conversation, I wondered why, if I enjoyed Mrs. Dent's company the few
times I had encountered it, I felt as I did. I told myself it was
because there was something predatory and desperate about her,
although I could tell she took great pains to disguise her need. Yet
there was nothing wrong with wanting friends and pursuing friend-
ships, I told myself, and Mrs. Dent and I were friends.

Suddenly I became aware that Miss Quay had asked me a question I had not entirely comprehended. "I'm sorry," I said. "Excuse
me?"

"I was only asking if you liked coffee."

I thought this an odd question, given the time of day. "I do," I said, "although after that fine tea—"

"No," said Miss Quay, laughing. "I wasn't suggesting we partake. I was asking because Uncle Roddy's house is above a coffee store and smells rather strongly of coffee, and if you didn't like coffee, you wouldn't stand a chance of liking the house."

"I like the smell of coffee even better than the taste," I said.

"Well, you'll soon get tired of it, I've no doubt. If you take the house," she added quietly, as if her speculation was indiscreet.

We approached the market square, which was still fairly full of commerce. We made our way diagonally through the market and out the far corner, and walked up a steep narrow street of cobblestones that was evidently intended only for pedestrians. Miss Quay stopped outside a small shop, from whence the smell of coffee emerged. "This is the store," she said. "The proprietor, Ali, is a lovely man. He's Egyptian. You're sure to like him. His wife is named Doris and she never speaks."

I looked into the store, which was dark and fragrant and devoid of human life. A small coffee bar occupied the front part, behind which was an emporium filled with sacks of coffee beans, most of them spilling over onto the stone floor. "You get to Uncle Roddy's through here," said Miss Quay, indicating a door in the wall. I followed her through this door down a narrow alley that smelled strongly of coffee and faintly of urine and into a small interior courtyard that contained some piles of garbage and more sacks of coffee. "Ali is supposed to keep this cleared out, but I suppose he's been lax without Uncle Roddy hollering at him. If it bothers you, keep after him. We go up here," she said, indicating a flight of stone steps that ascended the back of the building. The steps were steep and there was no handrail; I followed Miss Quay up them, onto a little landing outside a door. She knelt and felt beneath an urn planted with desiccated geraniums and withdrew a large key with which she unlocked the door. She held it open for me, but I said, "No. After you." She entered the room, and I followed.

It was a large, dark room, with a terra-cotta floor scattered with dhurries. Miss Quay crossed the floor and pulled aside a heavy curtain, allowing the light from the setting sun to enter the room and reveal its spaciousness. The walls and the beamed ceiling were spackled with some rough whitewashed material. The sofa and several chairs were made of wood and cushioned with a woven fabric that matched the rugs underfoot. Bookcases crammed with books lined one whole wall, from floor to ceiling, and piles of books were stacked in front of these cases, awaiting inclusion. Outside the window Miss Quay had revealed by opening the drapes was a large terrace with a small fountain at its center; it apparently functioned as an out-of-doors dining room as well, judging from the mosaic-topped table and chairs placed beside the fountain. The view from this terrace was spectacular: down over the roofs of the town — I could see my turret sticking up at the base of the hill — and out over the harbor.

"The kitchen's rather grungy and cramped," said Miss Quay, and opened a door to reveal a room that perfectly matched her description. "Uncle Roddy was a great one for eating out." She closed the door and then indicated a small enclosed staircase that rose steeply from an archway in the back of the room. "There's a bedroom and bath upstairs," she said. "I'll let you explore those yourself. My uncle had the bed shipped all the way from India. He claimed it was a maharajah's wedding bed, used only to consummate marriages. I suppose maharajahs married with some frequency."

I excused myself and ventured up the steps. The bedroom was as large as the living room. A huge four-poster bed, carved from teak and inlaid with mother-of-pearl, occupied the middle of the room. Instead of rising vertically, the posts ascended inwardly, intertwining themselves in the air high above the bed, four carved hands clasping one another's wrists, suspending a mosquito net from this considerable height.

One door revealed a walk-in closet full of neatly arranged suits and shoes; another a quite luxurious bathroom, which featured both a granite bathtub and a metal stall shower. The wall of windows downstairs was repeated upstairs, and these opened out onto a small narrow balcony, big enough for a chaise longue and a cocktail table, which looked down onto the terrace below and beyond that to the expanse of town and harbor. I stepped out onto the balcony and, leaning against the rail, noticed that Miss Quay was sitting on the terrace below me, on a chair drawn up alongside the parapet, looking out at the view. She had her elbow propped on the low wall and her chin in her hand, and something about her posture and attitude assured me that her face was once again veiled with sadness. I watched her for a moment as she sat there, hardly moving, regarding the vista, all of which was burnished now in the soft golden light of dusk, and I wanted to call out to her, to make her turn and look at me, as she had turned and looked when I had spoken to her on the lawn at Quayside; I wanted to watch her face perform that miraculous transformation I had earlier witnessed, but I did not know what to say: calling "Miss Quay" into the ambered evening air seemed not to suit the moment, and although her mother had called her Jean, I had not yet been introduced to her as Jean, so that name was out of the question. Finally I resorted to a rather stupid and desperate "Hello, down there."

She turned and looked up at me. Her face was streaked with tears. She raised a hand and wiped at her eyes. I was prepared for unhappiness implied, not unhappiness demonstrated: I knew not what to say or do. I felt as if I had interrupted somebody at something very private, for in my life emotion had always been something people had alone, or together in a bad way. I wasn't sure if I should leave her alone or go down to her. Fortunately, she recovered herself before I myself did.

"Forgive me," she said.

"Are you all right?" I stupidly asked, as if she had been hurt and was in need of first aid.

"Yes," she said, and then she repeated, more definitely, to convince herself: "Yes. I just weep from time to time," she said. "I'm — well, I can't explain it, so I won't attempt to. But how embarrassing for both of us. You must forgive me."

"There's nothing to forgive," I said. "Wait, I'll come down." I looked out at the harbor one last time and then withdrew into the room. I hurried down the steps, but Miss Quay was nowhere to be seen; the living room and the terrace were empty. I discovered her in the kitchen standing in front of the open refrigerator. Her eyes were dry and she wore a look of somewhat forced gaiety. She reached into it and withdrew a bottle of champagne, holding it out for me to see. "Look what Uncle Roddy left behind," she said. "Do you like champagne?"

I remember her asking me if I liked coffee and hoped that this question was less speculative. "Very much," I said. "Especially champagne as good as that."

She looked at the label. "Is it good? Then I suppose we should drink it, because champagne doesn't keep, does it?"

"Well, not forever," I said.

"And I need a drink, and I'm sure Uncle Roddy would like us to drink it. As a sort of baptism, or welcome. To transfer the spirit of domicile." She opened a cabinet and withdrew two champagne flutes. "They're a bit dusty," she said. "I'll rinse them out. You open this." She handed me the bottle of champagne. I ripped off the foil collar and untwined its wire harness, then eased the cork from the mouth of the bottle, and when it made that most satisfying sound of release, something inside me let go, opened, reoccurred, and I stood uncorked and allowed the wine to froth exuberantly over my hands as I felt the something inside me inflate, rushing from my heart in all directions, to the far-flung, impermeable borders of my body. It was the joy that comes from feeling you are where you should be.

CHAPTER SIX

1 HAD LUNCH WITH MRS. DENT AT THE CANTINA THE NEXT DAY. We ate outside this time, at one of the umbrella-shrouded tables, looking down at the harbor. Mrs. Dent was wearing a gaily patterned sundress that revealed more of her skin than I was accustomed to seeing and a hat with a wide, sloping brim that concealed her hair and, at certain moments, her face. Dino lay panting at our feet, attempting to curl his large body beneath our small table.

"Tell me about the Quays," I said, after we had ordered (sea bass for me; "as usual" for her).

"First you tell me about your visit."

"I enjoyed it," I said. "I think I'm going to rent this house they have. I went to see it after tea with Miss Quay."

"Jean or Nancy?"

"There are two Miss Quays?"

"Yes, and a brother, I believe, off somewhere in dubious but lucrative business—selling powdered baby formula to natives, something like that. Both sisters presently reside at Quayside. Jean is the dutiful, maiden daughter, and Nancy is the wild one: divorced two or three times, a bit of an alcoholic, a little crazy. But charming. And popular."

"I found Jean charming."

I could tell Mrs. Dent had raised her eyebrows; they disappeared beneath the brim of her hat. "Did you?" she said. "That's interesting. She's usually considered to be rather a dullard."

"No," I said. "I liked her very much. She's quiet, yes, but not dull." The waiter delivered our pitcher of wine and poured some into both our glasses. "What else can you tell me?"

"About the Quays?" said Mrs. Dent. She watched the wine settle into her glass. It seemed to have a slight effervescence. "Nothing really. They're just what they seem: a fine old family with lots of money. I understand Colonel Quay was a much admired statesman, but that was considerably before my time." She paused for a moment, looking at me, quite beautiful beneath the great brim of her hat, which set her face off, presented it, like a gift. "Listen," she said, "don't let . . ."

"What?"

"No. I shouldn't say anything."

"What were you going to say? Say it, please."

Mrs. Dent picked up a fork and examined its tines. It appeared as though she was counting them. "It's only—well, it will sound stupid of me, but why not?" She returned the fork to the table and looked at me. "Don't get too tight with them, is all. They'll take you over."

"What do you mean: take me over?"

"They're very controlling, socially. I'm speaking about Mrs. Quay, of course. She'll start organizing your social life. I'm sure she has her eye on you for Jean."

"You do? Really?"

"Oh, don't be dense, or naïve. I'm sure she wants you to marry Jean."

"That's absurd," I said. "She knows nothing about me. How does she even know I am eligible?"

"One naturally assumes a handsome young man traveling alone is unmarried. It is a truth universally acknowledged."

"Is it? Does one? Well, it's a foolish assumption. And I'm not a handsome young man."

"That's a matter of opinion," said Mrs. Dent. She touched her small pointed tongue to her lips for a moment, and then said, "Are you?"

"Am I what?"

"Don't be coy. Eligible."

"No," I said. "I am not eligible for marriage."

"So you are married?"

"Yes," I said. "In a manner of speaking."

"May I ask in what manner of speaking you are married?"

"I am separated from my wife," I said.

"Ah," said Mrs. Dent. "And you have left her behind? Or is she perhaps traveling on her own?"

It had not occurred to me to invent a traveling wife, but Mrs. Dent's suggestion of one seemed useful.

"Yes," I said.

"And where does she travel?"

"In the South Pacific," I said.

"Ah," Mrs. Dent repeated, with a calmness I found annoying, as if nothing I said could surprise her.

"She is interested in anthropology," I stupidly added.

"I'm sure she is," said Mrs. Dent. "What is her name?"

"Listen," I said, "I'm sure you'll understand if I don't want to talk about my wife. It's painful for me. The point of all this is that Mrs. Quay doesn't know me well enough to consider me a prospective son-in-law. I am a stranger to her."

"Sometimes strangers make the best relatives," said Mrs. Dent. "Especially in Andorra."

"What does that mean?"

"Only that in a country this small, strangers — newcomers — are attractive simply because they're unknown. As I'm sure you've noticed by now, everyone knows everyone else's business, and when you know too much about people, it can — well, the bloom is off the rose. Relatively little is known about you, and that's immensely appealing, because people can imagine all sorts of wonderful things."

"They could just as easily imagine not so wonderful things about me."

"They could, of course, but that isn't in their best interest. And people always do what is in their best interest."

"I think you're wrong about all this," I said. "Mrs. Quay is a very discerning woman who met me briefly for tea. She wouldn't push her daughter into a marriage with a dark horse like me. And Jean seems very much her own person. I'm sure she wouldn't allow herself to be pushed into anything by her mother."

"Well, it appears as though you're the expert on the Quays. If you know them so well, why even ask me about them in the first place?" Mrs. Dent turned to one side, crossed her legs, looked away.

The truth was, I had kissed Miss Quay the night before, outside
the Q-encrusted gates of Quayside.

As we drank the bottle of champagne on the terrace, the air
around us cooled. A coffee-scented breeze blew up from the street,
and the sky turned purple. We spoke quietly and mostly about her;
I asked her questions and she answered them hesitantly yet thoughtfully. Her answers were neither ready nor glib, and I realized she
was not in the habit of speaking about herself, and that many of
these ordinary questions had never been posed to her before.

I had succeeded in learning this about Miss Quay: That she had
been born at Quayside and grew up there, had gone to finishing
school in Switzerland at age sixteen, had spent two years at the
University of Lyon, had returned to Andorra at age twenty and lived
there ever since, except for a year or two in Ceylon with her Uncle
Demerest (now deceased). She was devoted to her mother and to
her four-year-old niece, Barbara, who was called Bitsy. She liked
the ballet but not the opera; her favorite authors were Jane Austen
and Daphne du Maurier.

After finishing the champagne, we left the little house, locking
it up behind us. She returned the key beneath the urn, and we
walked through the town, this time passing the hotel and crossing
the plaza. The fountain was lit from within so that the water pulsed
radiantly up into the darkening sky. The cantina was filling up for
the evening and I suggested we stop there for a drink, but Miss
Quay said no, that she had drunk more than enough for one evening, and anyway, her mother was bound to be anxious. So we
walked up the alley onto the dark peninsula road. The ancient trees

towered on either side of us, obscuring most of the sky except for a narrow furrow directly above our heads which was sown thickly with stars. As we walked, I looked up dizzily at this path of stars that mirrored the road we walked on. We arrived at Quayside and stopped outside the gates, which were closed, and stood for a moment in an awkward silence. We had barely talked on the walk back, but that silence had been agreeable, coupled as it was with the activity of walking. Now it was all we had: silence. And wind and stars. Miss Quay reached out a hand and clasped the gate, and in an effort to delay her disappearance, I asked her if she could identify the constellations. She told me no, but looked up at the sky anyway, as if this knowledge might suddenly come to her. By raising her face she exposed her long neck to the starlight, and almost without thinking (I was thinking, of course, but not in a way that controlled or even affected my actions) I reached out my hand and gently touched the cool skin of her neck. She looked at me for a moment, not with fear or surprise, as I expected, but with a strange calmness, and then she closed her eyes. My hand was still on her neck, and I was aware of her face moving toward mine, and I thought: I am about to kiss Miss Quay, and I felt a sort of wonderful terror that disappeared as our lips met.

Kissing someone for the first time is always a sort of miracle, an exhilarating journey up a strange river over rapids.

The journey completed, we stood for a moment, returned to our original awkward silence. Finally Miss Quay held out her hand and said good evening.

I shook her hand and watched her open the gates and then close them, obscuring herself behind the scrim of night and Qs.

"Let's not talk about the Quays," Mrs. Dent was saying. "It's stupid to. They're bound to come between us and make things rotten."

"Why should they come between us?" I asked.

"Oh," she said, sounding exasperated, "because they do and they will, and I don't want to talk about it. It's dreary. I'm sorry I brought them up. How's your fish?"

"Delicious. How is your 'as usual'?"

"As usual," said Mrs. Dent. "Tell me, when are you planning to move?"

"Not for a few days. I've taken my hotel room for the week."

"I want to come up and see it. I've only seen the public rooms in the Hotel Excelsior, but I've heard the guest rooms are really something. Is yours? Do you have a suite? If I had my way I would live in hotels. I adore them."

"I've got a nice room stuck way up in the turret, with a little balcony wrapped around the outside. The view is marvelous."

"Can we go up? After lunch?"

"I don't know," I said. "It seems a very proper hotel. I haven't had any visitors, and I think they'd frown on me bringing ladies back to my room."

"Andorra isn't as quaint as you apparently think. They've seen it all at the Excelsior, I'm sure. In any case, it's the middle of the day! It's quite decent to have friendly visitors in the afternoon."

The prospect of being alone in my hotel room with Mrs. Dent both frightened and excited me. Unfortunately one sensation refused to take precedent. "What about Dino?" I lamely asked.

"Dino's a very well-behaved dog. He's stayed in finer hotels than the Excelsior, in fact. I just want to come up for a look."

"I was going to explore the town a bit after lunch," I said.

"Oh, please. You have the rest of your life to explore the town. In case you haven't noticed, it's a very small town in a very small country. Pace yourself. Save something for later, for God's sake. Now eat your fish."

Mrs. Dent was right: my taking her up to my room disturbed no one at the Hotel Excelsior. Dino's hugeness prevented him from climbing the spiral staircase, so Mrs. Dent commanded him to lie down and stay, and knotted his leash around the newel. I led my guest up the staircase and paused at the top, to unlock the door. "How thrilling," I heard Mrs. Dent whisper from behind me, and I wasn't sure what exactly thrilled her: the prospect of seeing the hotel room or the prospect of being alone in it with me.

I opened the door and stepped aside on the small landing at the top of the stairs. As she passed by me, I smelt an intoxicating mix of warm skin, powder, fragrance, and a trace of perspiration, and I could feel the warmth of her body.

She removed her hat and stood in the alcove just inside the door, surveying the room. It looked much as I had seen it on that first day: suffused with sun, every object poised and bathed with light, the filmy curtains susurrating at the window, some papers rustling on the desk. "It's perfect," Mrs. Dent said, after a moment. "It's so lovely I could cry." She crossed to the balcony doors and looked outside. "You're up so high, and with this gorgeous light all around

you. It's like being held up in God's hands, or something, isn't it?"
She looked over at me.

"I've never thought of it that way," I said. I remained standing
by the door, as if afraid to actually be in the same room with her.

"You should," she said. "It is God's room. A room of God. It's
funny, I never feel religious or even think about God in churches,
but in a room like this I could believe in God easily and happily.
Luxury hotels are the real houses of God, I think. Hotels and mu-
seums." She walked about the room, looking at and touching the
furniture, picking up and palming one of the alabaster eggs, and
then she studied the mural. "You see," she said, "I was right: the
room is blessed. Jeanne d'Arc is my favorite saint." She kissed her
fingertips and then reached up and touched the hem of the visionary Joan's dress. "And look," she said, pointing to the prie-dieu,
which stood beside me in the alcove. "You even have something
to pray on." My journal was resting in its place upon the little
alabastered shelf of the altar, and she came over and picked it up.
"What's this?" she said.

"It's nothing," I said, taking it from her.

"What do you mean nothing? It's obviously something."

"It's my journal."

"Oh! How sweet. The one you bought the other day, at Krie-
gelstein's?"

"Yes," I said.

"And you pray to it?"

"No," I said. "I write in it."

"Would you read me a bit?"

"No," I said.

"Let me see it," she said, "just the outside." She reached out her hand, and I gave it to her. She stroked the fabric of the cover and said, "It's beautiful." Then, glancing at me, she opened the book. "I'm not going to read it," she said. "I promise you. I just want to look at it. My, what forceful handwriting you have." She closed the book, returned it to its stand, and then walked over to the balcony doors. This time she stepped out into the sunlight. After a moment, she looked back into the room. "Come out," she called.

I joined her on the balcony. The day was radiant and the town seemed to be jeweled. It almost hurt to look at it: the sparkling aquamarine harbor, the diamondiferous fountain—everything brilliantly illuminated by the indiscriminate sun. We stood for a moment, our arms on the railing, blinking down at the view. "I like Andorra from up here," said Ricky. "I think it's a nicer place to look at than to live in."

"I enjoy both," I said.

"That is the privilege of the newcomer. Enjoy it while you can."

"I intend to," I said. "But do you think you'd be happier someplace else?"

"Wouldn't we all?" she said with a laugh. "I at least like to think so. But of course not. One thing I've learned is that one's happiness—or unhappiness—is internal, and we carry it about with us, from place to place. Like a turtle carries his shell."

"A change of scene often changes one's mood," I said.

"Briefly, perhaps, and superficially, but not in any real or lasting way." She was leaning on the rail, resting her chin in her hands, looking down at the town. And then she suddenly stood up straight and clapped her hands and said, "Well. I'd better retrieve my dog and head home. I'll leave you to your siesta. You do take a siesta, don't you? It's too lovely a room not to nap in."

"Sometimes I lie down for a little while in the afternoon."

"American men are so embarrassed about napping," she said. "They think it is some sort of feminine indulgence. I detest a man who can't nap."

I walked her to the door of the room. She loitered for a moment in the little alcove, running her finger over the cover of my journal, tracing the batiked pattern of the fabric. "Will you tell me something?" she asked.

"What?" I asked.

"Why did you lie to me before?"

"When?" I asked.

"At the cantina," she said. "I know you lied about your wife."

I had opened the door, but now I closed it. "Yes," I said. "I did lie to you."

"Why?"

I shrugged. "I lied to you because I did not want to tell you the truth," I said.

"Yes," she said. "Of course."

We were silent a moment. "You should learn to tell the truth," she said, "or improve your lies."

"I like my lies," I said.

"Why? They are remarkably unconvincing."

"How do you know?" I asked.

She looked at me. Her expression alarmed me: she looked genuinely disturbed. "Oh," she said. "You mean that you've told me others. Have you?"

"Maybe," I said.

"So I am to believe nothing you say."

"You can believe everything I say. If you choose to."

"I'm sorry," she said. "But I don't accept that burden. I'd rather you said nothing to me than to lie." She put on her hat, and then she reached out to open the door, but I held it shut with my hand.

For a moment we stood there in the alcove. She let go of the doorknob and looked down at her feet. The floor of the alcove was a mosaic of little tiles: inside a wreath, two beady-eyed doves held a garland in their beaks, and on the garland was the motto IN LIMINE.

"My wife is dead," I said. "Both my wife and my daughter are dead. They died in an accident."

She looked up at me. "I'm so sorry," she said.

"It's why I've come here," I said. "I couldn't stay where I was. There seemed to be no possible life for me there."

"Yes," she said. "I understand. You were right to come away."

"I'm sorry I lied before," I said. "I hope you'll forgive me."

"Of course I do," she said. "You're all right now, aren't you?" She reached out and touched my arm.

"Of course I am," I said.

"Then I'll let you take your nap. And I'll talk to you soon, I hope."

I stood at the top of the staircase and watched her descend. Dino sat up and also watched her, and there was something odd about the symmetry of it: me at the top looking down, Dino at the bottom looking up, and Mrs. Dent spiraling down between us.

I closed the door and stood in the center of my room, looking around it as Ricky Dent had. The curtains still fluttered at the window, but the light had altered, dimmed a bit, for the apex of the afternoon had been achieved and relinquished, and in that relinquishment I sensed a larger, more permanent abandonment. I felt very keenly the inherent sadness of late afternoon.

CHAPTER SEVEN

I DON'T KNOW HOW LONG I STOOD IN MY ROOM AFTER MRS.
Dent left. I suppose I was in a sort of daze, thinking: Will this
work? I was afraid of making another mistake, for I knew how easily
mistakes can lead to tragedy, and I wanted to avoid all that, I wanted
to be smart and clear and lead a bright, clean, good, fine life. In
Andorra.

This reverie was interrupted—no, terminated—by a knock at the
door. I felt trapped, and decided to feign absence, for a knock on
the door invariably leads to something larger and more complicated
than a knock on the door, and I wasn't sure I was ready for anything
large and complicated.

Sometimes it is necessary to stay still in one's life.

The knock was repeated, and a man's voice—it sounded like the
valet's—said my name dully and uninquiringly, as if he was reading
it from a list. I did not answer. I was standing perfectly still and
sweating, staring at the door as if it might explode, as if storm
troopers might batter it down. As I watched the door a slip of paper
appeared beneath it: slowly at first, almost threateningly, and then,
with an apparent tap, it slid a few inches into the alcove. I heard
feet descend the staircase, and then all was silent.

I felt relieved, for I had avoided the interaction threatened by

the knock, but the slip of paper lying just inside the door was trouble-
some. It was not a person, for which I was grateful, but it troubled
me almost as much as the knock, for of course it implied a person.

I decided to take a nap before I read what was on the paper. And
I felt much better as soon as I lay on the bed. Sometimes it is a
bad thing to stand up too long, thinking. At least it is for me. It
was as if by standing up I could see all the problems around me,
but lying down changed the perspective and all these problems
disappeared. All I could see was the conical ceiling of the turret,
the beautifully simple symmetry of it: rising into a single point. A
single point: the house of God.

When I woke from my nap I glanced over at the door. The slip
of paper was still there, and as I thought *still there*, I realized I had
half hoped or expected that it might disappear.

I got down from the bed and walked over and picked up a single
sheet of hotel stationery folded in half, with my name hurriedly
scrawled on the outside.

I unfolded the sheet and read the following message:

> Dinner tonight? I hope you'll come. I know it's short notice, but
> I suspect you're free, and I think it's time you meet my husband.
> Nothing formal or stuffy—just a nice meal (well, I'll try!) with
> me and Ricky. If you're one of those Americans who feel obli-
> gated to turn up with wine or flowers, don't. Just come about
> eight—or earlier if you'd like. We're at No. 14 Auguste Beernaert
> (on the fourth terrace); ask at the desk for directions.

It was signed Fondly, Ricky. I said the word out loud, to myself:
Fondly. It sounded odd.

The Dent house was situated at the end of a quiet cul-de-sac. I arrived a little after eight o'clock; the light was just beginning to fade, and in this twilight the house looked inanimate, like a beloved and slightly sentimental picture of itself. It was a small, snug house of only two stories, with unfaded red granite walls and a mossy slate roof. It appeared to be empty, although several windows were open and I could hear music coming from somewhere nearby. I walked up the herringbone brick walk and knocked at the door, which was covered by a little latticed porch, over which swarmed papaya-colored bougainvillaea. No one answered my knock. I waited a moment or two and then stepped off the porch and followed the brick walk around the side of the house to a low stone wall with a wooden gate. From here I could see into the tiny back garden, which was completely walled. A small manicured lawn was bordered by flowering shrubs. A stone birdbath stood in the middle of the lawn, with an inch of silvery water in its basin, and in the far corner of the yard was a gazebo, with a peaked roof and screened-in sides. It was from here that the music originated, and as I stood at the gate I heard talk and laughter as well. I raised the latch and opened the gate and stepped onto the lawn, and as I did this, a little bell attached to the gate tinkled. Dino emerged from the shrubs, barking across the lawn. The screen door of the little house opened and Ricky Dent—Mrs. Ricky Dent—emerged. She clapped her hands and called Dino's name; he barked once or twice more and then sat down.

"You've come!" cried Mrs. Dent, her hands clasped in her final clap. "I'm so happy." She crossed the lawn and kissed me on my cheek. "We're just having a drink in the summerhouse. Come and join us."

I followed her across the lawn. She held open the door of the tiny house and I entered ahead of her, stepping up onto the wooden platform. A wrought-iron bench encircled the small room. In the middle of the floor was a round table shrouded in white linen on which rested a silver wine bucket, filled with icy water and a bottle of wine, several guttering candles, and an old wind-up Victrola playing what sounded like Mozart. As I entered, a man sitting on the bench stood up and held out his hand. He was very tall and blond, with shining eyes and teeth. His handshake was warm and strong. "I'm so glad to meet you," he said. "I'm Ricky Dent."

I told him I was glad to meet him, too.

"Would you like a glass of wine?" he asked.

"Please," I said. I sat on the bench. Mrs. Dent sat across from me, and we both watched Mr. Dent pour my wine. "Cheers," he said as he handed it to me. "Welcome to Andorra."

"Thank you," I said. I realized I had been worried about meeting Mr. Dent—I had presumed him to be an ornery character, for some reason—but my worries were unfounded. I liked this man instinctively and immediately: there was something warm and unthreatening about him.

"Are the bugs out?" asked Mrs. Dent.

"I didn't notice them," I said.

"Perhaps we should sit on the terrace, then. Do you think it's gloomy in here?"

"Not at all," I said.

"Ricky's told me lots about you," said Mr. Dent, as he sat beside his wife. He put his arm around her in a gesture that seemed a little unnatural and consciously illustrative. "I'm glad she's found someone to lunch with. I got bored with the cantina, you see. And I found that lunching out interrupts my day. I can never return to work afterwards. I always want to sleep, or walk, or, worst of all, just keep drinking. And that's no good."

"No," I said.

"Ricky's writing an opera," said Mrs. Dent. "That's why I don't feel bad, leaving him alone all afternoon. In fact, I think he quite likes it. Don't you, darling?"

"I don't mind being solitary. But I always find myself looking forward to your return."

"Are you a composer?" I asked.

"An amateur one," he answered. "I love music, and played the English horn semiprofessionally in the New South Wales Chamber Orchestra. So when we moved here I decided I needed an ambitious project to keep me out of trouble. Writing an opera seemed pretty damn ambitious, and it's certainly kept me occupied."

"Is it an original story?" I asked.

"Lord, no," he said. "I'm not creative that way in the slightest. I'm adapting Gide's *The Immoralist*. Very freely adapting it, I should say."

"It's quite good," said Mrs. Dent. "We're hoping the Andorran National Opera will put it up when Ricky's finished."

"No, we aren't," said Mr. Dent. "And it isn't good at all."

"Well, *I* do hope," said Mrs. Dent. "And it *is* good."

"Do you like music?" asked Mr. Dent.

"I'm afraid I am hopelessly unmusical," I said. "In fact, almost tragically unmusical."

"Tragically?" asked Mrs. Dent. "That's saying a lot. How tragically?"

"It has stopped me from believing in God," I said.

"Really? Why?"

"I love to sing. Or I did. When I was growing up I loved to sing. But I'm an awful singer. I remember in grade school the music teacher wrote on my report that, while I was an enthusiastic singer, I 'was unable to cope with the pitch.' I had to ask my mother to explain to me what that meant, and my mother said it meant I sang loudly and badly. I was devastated."

"And that prevented you from believing in God?"

"I've always thought it has, in a way. I suppose it was the first time I doubted His existence. It just suddenly seemed very clear to me: if God existed He would have given me the ability to sing beautifully — or at least competently — because I liked to sing so much."

"But there are many things we want to be able to do that we cannot do, for one reason or another," said Mrs. Dent. "I'm sure God granted you other talents."

"Yes, I'm sure He did," I said. "It's just that growing up, back then, it seemed very cruel that I couldn't cope with the pitch. I felt silenced, somehow, in a way that seemed extremely uncharitable. I've never felt comfortable singing publicly after that. It's sad, what can happen, when we realize we are not perceived as we think we are. You see, I always thought I was a wonderful singer. In my head I heard myself that way."

"Then I'm sure you can sing," said Mr. Dent. "No one's tone-deaf. It's just a matter of learning how to hear music differently. It's all in the ears. And I'm sure you aren't half as bad a singer as you think."

"People don't sing very much anymore, do they?" said Mrs. Dent. "People sing when they're alone, or think they're alone, but didn't people used to sit together in the evening and sing? Before the awful nuisance of radio and television? Did they? Or am I just being romantic?"

"I believe so," said her husband. "Singing was a social activity. Young ladies learned how to play the piano and sing. And singing was a quality valued in men as well."

"It's really quite sad, when you think about it," said Mrs. Dent. "I mean, I'm trying to think of a song I know all the way through: you know, a proper song, a song I could get up and sing, and I can't think of any. Do you know what I think I'll do? I'm going to plan an evening of song. You can play the piano, Ricky, and we can all sing. I'll buy some sheet music so we can follow along. And you must come, Mr. Fox, and sing with us. I'm sure in a group you'll sing quite well."

"Why would I sing any better in a group?" I asked.

"I don't know why, I just feel you will," said Mrs. Dent. "Ricky darling, wind the gramophone. It's slowing." She was right: the music was slurred and slowed, as if the orchestra were climbing up a mountain as they played.

Mr. Dent cranked the handle of the record player, and the music suddenly sounded brighter. We all listened to it, glad, I think, for the distraction. I looked through the screen onto the lawn. A bird was fluttering its wings in the birdbath, splashing the silvery water out onto the grass.

Mrs. Dent stood and put her empty wineglass on the table. The bowl of it was rinsed with traces of wine, and glowed a little in the candlelight. "I'll go see to our dinner," she said. "I won't be a moment."

She opened the door and stepped out onto the lawn. The bird flew up from the basin, into the darkening sky. Dino roused himself from the hedges and followed his mistress into the house. And so I was left alone with Mr. Dent. He was sitting across from me, in the candlelit gloom of the summerhouse. For a moment we just looked at one another, then Mr. Dent stood up and pulled the bottle of wine from the bucket. He crossed the room and sat down next to me and topped off my glass. The bottle was wet from its icy bath and some water dripped from it onto my pant leg. I felt the dots of cold on my thigh, pinpricks of sensation that burned for a second before fading. I tried to think of something to say to Mr. Dent, but I could think of nothing. I sipped at my wine and then said, "How far along are you with your opera?"

"I've finished a draft of the libretto," he said. "And I have about a third of it very roughly scored."

"What an interesting project."

"Ricky tells me you're writing a book," he said.

"Not really a book. It's only a journal."

"Oh. Ricky thought it was a book. A novel."

"I wouldn't presume to write a novel," I said. It sounded so fey and self-indulgent, and I did not want to be in the same class as Mr. Ricky Dent, spending his afternoons writing an opera no one would ever hear. I tried to remember what *The Immoralist* was about, but came up with nothing, except for a dim memory of heat and disease. Africa?

"Do you think it takes presumption to write a novel?" he asked.

"Well, for me it would, I think. I'm not a real writer."

"I suppose, as I'm not a real composer, it's presumptuous of me to write an opera," he said. "It's funny, but I've never thought of it in those terms before. And I have to say I'm glad I haven't, because it probably would have stopped me, and I've been enjoying myself, so it would have been a shame."

"Yes," I said. His guilelessness was charming, but I was a little angry with him, for I felt I had been made to look a fool.

We were silent a moment.

"I'm sorry about dripping the water on your trousers," he said in a sudden gruff way. "I should have wrapped the bottle with a towel."

"Oh, it's fine," I said. "It's quite dry, in fact." I nodded down at my pants, and then rubbed at the few moist spots.

"I could lend you a pair of dry trousers, if you'd like."

"That's kind of you, but these are fine," I said.

"No hard feelings?" he asked.

I thought this conversation was rather insane, but Mr. Dent seemed perfectly serious. "Of course not," I said. "It was nothing."

He stood up and put the wine back into the bucket, and stirred the icy water with it, round and round. "You're a very decent man," he said, looking down into the bucket. "I know you're friends with Ricky, but I do hope we can be friends, too."

I wondered why everyone in Andorra was so desperate for friend-ship. Or maybe it was just the Dents: the poor, lonely, demented Dents.

"Perhaps I can work with you on your singing," he was saying. "I'm sure I could help you cope with the pitch."

I didn't really want to have singing lessons with Mr. Dent, so I didn't answer. He had created a little whirlpool in the bucket. He lifted the bottle out and watched the water swirl. After a moment the current abated and he resettled the bottle. "I'll sing a note, and then you try to match it," he said, still looking down into the bucket. Without waiting for my reply he sang "Laaaaa." His singing voice was beautiful: pure and unwavering.

"I can't sing," I said.

"Of course you can," he said. "Try it. Laaaaa."

I shook my head. "I'd rather not," I said. "I'm a little self-conscious about my voice."

"But that's a shame," he said, finally looking at me. "That's prob-ably your problem: that self-consciousness interferes with your true voice, distorts it."

"Perhaps," I said.

"There's no reason for you to be embarrassed with me," he said.

I didn't answer.

"Laaaaa," he sang. The same note, but quietly.

I tried to duplicate the sound. The pitch seemed right to me, but then it always does. My voice itself sounded feeble, wavering.

"That wasn't bad," he said. "Close your eyes. No, really: close them."

I closed my eyes.

"Now listen: Laaaaa."

On the dark screen of my eyelids I saw a great veldt silhouetted against a sky streaked with blue and orange light. "Laaaaa," I sang.

"Perfect," he said. "Keep your eyes closed. Listen." He sang: " 'Down yonder . . .' "

Something was lumbering slowly across my veldt: a tank or an elephant.

" 'Down yonder . . .' " he repeated.

I sang those words, and then he sang the next phrase, which I tried to mimic, and we continued in this fashion until he said, "Good. Don't open your eyes. Now the whole thing: 'Down yonder green valleys, where streamlets meander, where twilight is fading, I pensively roam.' "

I closed my eyes tighter. The veldt narrowed, then disappeared. It was just black now. I sang the line, more slowly than Mr. Dent. When I was finished I heard someone — not Mr. Dent — say, "That was lovely." I opened my eyes. Mrs. Dent was standing just outside the screen door. Her face was obscured by the darkness and the screen, and for a moment I didn't recognize her. For a moment I forgot where I was. It seemed to have gotten darker while I had my eyes closed: the candlelight was brighter, its shadow flickering on our faces and across the ceiling.

Mrs. Dent opened the door, revealing herself, but remained outside. A moth flew into the room and made straight for the guttering candle. "You *can* sing!" she said. "That was lovely."

We had dinner in the summerhouse, an endearingly awful dinner of soggy quiche Lorraine, a salad of tinned beets and hearts of palm, and one of those revolting rolled cakes filled with jam, sprinkled with sugared coconut, and doused with kirsch.

We were sitting in the Dents' small but comfortable living room, drinking brandy, when a clock chimed from somewhere down the dark hallway and Mrs. Dent said, "Goodness, it's late. I'm going to abandon the two of you. I have my animals in the morning."

"What animals?" I asked.

"I do my civil service at the animal rescue shelter. I'm a trained veterinary doctor."

"What civil service?"

"Oh? Didn't you know. All Andorran citizens are expected to provide six hours of civil service a week. I'm sure once you start renting a house, they'll come after you. I spend two mornings a week at the shelter."

"What do you do?" I asked Mr. Dent.

"I teach music to schoolchildren in a village up on the Vega," he said.

"Is it obligatory?" I asked.

"Not really," said Mrs. Dent. "They don't fine or imprison you if you don't contribute. But most people do. It makes things better, and keeps taxes down. Andorra has the lowest taxes of any developed nation, you know."

"I didn't know."

"Didn't you? That's why most people move here."

"What other things can you do?"

"In the civil service? Just about anything. People invent things to suit themselves. Clarissa Sanjuro does the flowers in the municipal building, for instance. Brings them in from her garden two mornings a week. What did you do in the States? Did you have a profession?"

"Several," I said. "Most recently I owned a bookstore."

"Then you could work in the Biblioteca. A lot of the bookish people do that."

"The Biblioteca. Is that a library?"

"Not really. It's more a nationally subsidized bookstore. You can buy books there or exchange them. They have some elaborate system I've never understood. We buy our books at The House of Mirth. They have the best selection of English titles."

"Where's the Biblioteca?"

She told me it was in the building behind the municipal building, beside the spa, which I had not known existed. Other public amenities included a beach club, out at the tip of the peninsula. "You'll have to come with me some morning," said Mrs. Dent. "Do you like to swim?"

"Yes," I said, "very much."

"It gets a bit crowded in the afternoon, but it's quite nice in the morning. And the water's cooler then, too. I go out very early. Before breakfast, sometimes. I like to go for a morning swim and then have breakfast at the cantina." She fake-yawned, stood up, and said, "Well, as I said, I'm off to bed. Hillary comes in the morning, so you can leave the dishes, darling. I'm sure I'll see you soon, Mr. Fox. Thank you for coming."

I stood up and we exchanged good nights. And then she disappeared down the dark hall, in the direction of the chiming clock.

For a moment Mr. Dent and I sipped our brandies in silence, regarding the amber liquid with feigned interest. I knew it was late, but I was curiously in no rush to depart. It was nice to be in a home: the small warm rooms, the dark hall, the chiming clock, the open windows, the thick summery trees outside murmuring: safety, safety. The feeling of someone in another part of the house, readying herself for bed. It had been a long time since I had been in a calm home, late at night. I thought of the dark solitary walk back to the hotel and my room there, high and lonely, not even touching another room, and it seemed to me too much like my life.

I said to Mr. Dent, "I appreciate what you did before. Before dinner. Getting me to sing. That was very — I don't know — pleasurable for me. Thank you."

He reached out and put his brandy on the table. "You're welcome," he said.

"I don't want to keep you from joining your wife," I said. "It's late. I should go."

"No," he said. "I don't want — I mean, finish your drink, and then I'll walk you home. I've got to take Dino out anyway."

"Are you sure?" I said.

"Yes," he said. "I always walk Dino before bed."

We finished our brandies. Mr. Dent leashed Dino and we began walking down toward the hotel. The night was warm but windy. The trees made a great show of tossing their limbs in the air, like tempestuous, newly beautiful adolescents. Mr. Dent led me down the narrowest, steepest streets, and from behind the shuttered windows above us I could hear faint music, faint laughter.

"I understand my wife visited your hotel room this afternoon," Mr. Dent said suddenly. He tugged on Dino's leash. "Don't pull, Dino," he said.

I allowed as she had.

"She said it was very beautiful."

It sounded to me as if he was fishing for an invitation for himself, but I had had enough of the Dents for one day, so I didn't answer.

"I don't know if you made love to her or not," said Mr. Dent. "I assume you did."

"You assume incorrectly," I said.

He looked at me again. "Do you want to?" he asked. His tone was not accusing; it was merely curious.

"Why are you asking me these embarrassing questions?"

"I think it would be embarrassing if I didn't ask them," said Mr. Dent. "If we are to be friends. Are we to be friends?"

"I hope so," I said, thinking: This absurd rush toward friendship! As if we must all pair off before the imminent end of the world.

"Then I will say this, and without embarrassment: Ricky and I have an unusual marriage. I suppose every marriage is unusual, so that's not saying much. But you should know that if you were to sleep with Ricky, it would in no way affect our marriage. And it would in no way jeopardize our friendship."

We descended another flight of steps and walked down a quiet street of darkened shops. Each window we passed revealed another artfully arranged display of fruit or fish or fabric: gorgeous dioramas of commerce. "There's the Biblioteca," said Mr. Dent, nodding at a large building across the street. And then we came out onto the plaza, which we crossed. We stopped in front of the hotel and stood outside the revolving glass door, which, since it was late, was not revolving. Through the door I could see the deserted hotel lobby. It had a quiet air of abandonment: the valets stood about, as impassive as mannequins.

Mr. Dent looked out at the harbor, through the row of palm trees. And then he turned his head quickly toward me and said, "I think my wife is a little bit in love with you." He said this confidingly, not accusingly.

"I don't pretend to know the heart of your wife."

"Do you think we could go up to your room?" he asked me. "It's a bit awkward, isn't it, standing out here in the street?"

"I'm very tired," I said. "And it's awfully late. Perhaps—"

Mr. Dent laid his hand on my arm. The sudden warmth of it silenced me. "Please," he said. "Just for a moment."

My room was dark and a little chilly; I went about lighting lamps and closing windows, happy for this business, since being alone in the room with Mr. Dent slightly unnerved me. And then the room was cozy and bright, and I motioned for Mr. Dent to seat himself in a chair and sat down opposite him, on a small velvet fainting couch. We had said nothing to one another as I readied the room, and we sat in silence, awaiting the arrival of the brandy I had asked to be sent up. Soon it arrived, and was poured, and our positions were reassumed.

This is getting tedious, I thought, sipping my brandy, but as Mr. Dent had been the one intent on prolonging our meeting, I was determined to make him take the initiative. He sat forward, his legs apart, his elbows resting on his knees, regarding the floor.

"How's the brandy?" I asked.

"Fine," he said abruptly, and then sipped it, as if to make sure. "Very good," he said.

"It seems to me that it's you who wants to say something to me," I said.

"Does it?" he asked.

"Yes," I said.

"I suppose you're right," he said.

Suddenly I was enjoying myself. It had something to do with the extreme malleableness, the docility, the terrible lostness of Mr. Dent. I realized that he was more lost than I. And my pleasure in that fact was as keen as it was mean, for the disquieting truth is that other people's misery is often therapeutic. Whatever it was that had brought him to Andorra was more disruptive than what had brought me. He had not landed on his feet. He was a turtle on its back, waving its tiny feet in the air, writing an opera.

"What do you want to say to me?" I asked him.

He was looking into his glass of brandy, and I thought: The reason men drink is that they can't bear to look at one another when they speak; they need something to distract them. I rolled the brandy in my glass and took a sip.

Finally he looked up at me. "I wonder if Ricky . . ." he began.

"If Ricky what? Talk to me," I said.

"If Ricky told you anything about why we left Sydney. Why we came here."

"I believe she said fate brought you here. In the same way it has brought everyone here. Myself included."

He violently rubbed his lips with his fingers and then licked them, as if they had been stuck shut and prevented him from talking. Lips thus limbered, he said, "I love my wife."

I neither challenged nor affirmed this statement.

He glanced over at me, as if to make sure I hadn't fallen asleep. I raised my eyebrows to show that I was listening, and then he returned his attention to his brandy. "The problem is, in case you haven't noticed, I'm also attracted to men."

"Are you?" I said.

"Yes." He said it again, quietly: "Yes."

"Is that a problem?" I asked.

He gave an odd sudden shrug, as if repelling an insect that had alighted on his flesh, and said, "Yes."

"I'm sorry to hear that," I said. And I was. Poor Mr. Dent.

"Sorry to hear what?" he asked.

"That it's a problem," I said.

"Are you sorry to hear that I'm attracted to men?"

"No," I said. "Why should I be?"

He looked at me. "Because I am attracted to you." I realized how brave he was, and I was a little ashamed. It was my turn to study my brandy.

"You don't know what it's like," I heard him say. "I go on in my life, I try to—to, well, do the right thing, stupid as that sounds, but I try to live a life with decency and meaning, and then someone like you appears and it all falls away, and I'm left with nothing but thinking that everything I've done is wrong. Everything. Every single thing."

"Surely not everything," I said.

"What?" he asked.

"I said surely not everything. I mean, I do understand how you feel. In a way I do. To a certain extent. And I mean, well, surely there are many things you've done with your life that are right. You can't have done everything wrong. For instance, what about your opera?"

"My opera is terrible," he moaned. "It's all pretentious caterwauling."

"Well, I don't believe you. I simply can't believe you. You made me sing before. You did that. That wasn't wrong, was it?"

"No," he said. "But that was about you, mostly. That wasn't about me."

"It was very much about you," I said. "Of course it was about you. It was all about you."

"Oh God," he said. He put his glass down on the floor and covered his eyes with his fingers. "This is really pathetic, isn't it?"

"Nothing human is pathetic," I said, wondering where that was from. Tennessee Williams?

He took his hands away from his eyes and looked at me. "I don't know why I've told you all this. Exposed you to this. It's just that I have this loneliness, this awful, awful loneliness, and I become inured to it, and it doesn't even seem like loneliness anymore, for months on end it can weigh on me without my feeling it, and then something happens — like meeting you — and suddenly there's this weight, some awful mean alchemy that makes that loneliness assume weight, and I think it will crush me. That I will die. Or do something unspeakably violent."

"There's no need for you to suffer like that," I said.

"What do you mean?" he asked.

"I only mean that in this day and age there is no reason for you to suffer as you do."

"But what should I do?" he asked.

"I don't know," I said. "You must figure that out yourself. Make some arrangement with your wife. But you shouldn't suffer."

He stood up and walked to the balcony door, which I had left partially open. The breeze entered it determinedly, as if it would not be refused entrance. It ruffled Mr. Dent's blond hair. "I know that you're right," he said. "I'm weak in some way, some fatal way, that doesn't allow me to pursue my life." He shook his head. "Other people pursue their lives. You're doing that, I can tell. Yet I can't."

"I disagree," I said. "What are you doing now? Right now? Saying these things to me? Isn't that pursuing your life?"

"But nothing will come of it," said Mr. Dent. He turned away from the French doors and looked at me. "Will it?"

I stood up and put my glass down on a table. I walked over and stood beside him, looking out the doors. Very little was left lit. It wasn't really a city, I realized: everyone did go to bed at some point. And it wasn't so very late. I put my hand on his shoulder. "It's very late," I said. "You should go home."

"Yes," he said.

"We can be friends," I said. With my hand on his shoulder, I led him to my door and bade him good night.

Before undressing for bed I stepped out onto my balcony. The cantina was closed and the plaza was deserted, save for one person sitting on the rim of the fountain's large basin, looking up toward my turret. I could make out the large animal hunkered at its feet. I did not know if Mr. Dent could see me, but he looked up at me as if he could. For a very long time he looked up at me, as if he expected me to wave or throw down my key. Or jump.

As I watched, the fountain transformed itself: the lights turned off and the water ceased cascading. It was suddenly very quiet, and I realized what a noise the fountain made.

I remembered the tranquil bowl of silvered water in the Dents' birdbath.

I looked at my watch: Midnight.

CHAPTER EIGHT

*1*WAS AWOKEN EARLY THE NEXT MORNING BY A KNOCKING. I SAT up in bed and looked at the door. "Yes?" I called out.

"I have a note for you, sir," the valet said.

"Slip it under the door," I said.

"An answer is requested."

I looked at the clock on the bedside table: it was a few minutes past eight. I got out of bed and opened the door. The valet stood there in his absurd costume, all brass buttons and epaulets, with a note on a silver salver. He looked ridiculous, but I did not feel sorry for him. I grabbed the note from the tray and read it.

Dear Mr. Fox—I am sorry to disturb you, but it is absolutely necessary that I talk to you immediately about a serious matter. Will you please join me in the concierge's office as soon as possible? Your cooperation is appreciated.

It was signed: *Sincerely, Vladimir Afgroni,* and beneath that, carefully printed in block capital letters, was: LIEUTENANT, LA PLATA MUNICIPAL POLICE SQUADRON.

I could tell by the way the valet regarded me that he had read the note. I replaced it on the tray and said, "Tell Lieutenant Afgroni I will be with him shortly."

"Very well, sir," the valet said. He left.

I stood for a moment in the empty room. I felt panicked. What could have gone wrong? Perhaps the Dents were criminals of some sort. It would go a long way in explaining their aggressive decency and friendliness. I decided I was finished with them. I would get myself out of whatever jam they had gotten me in and never see them again. I had made a false start with the Dents. I would begin all over again.

I hurriedly dressed in the clothes that I had discarded the night before. They smelt of me in a not unpleasant way I found comforting, yet nevertheless I splashed on some cologne.

In the lobby I felt everyone peering at me from behind the splayed wings of their newspapers, but I knew I was being paranoid. I walked calmly across the large room to the reception desk. "Good morning," I said to the clerk who stood behind it, bracing himself with both arms against the polished wood. "I am looking for Lieutenant Afgroni."

"Yes, Mr. Fox," he said. "He is waiting for you. Right this way." He motioned me behind the counter and I followed him down a hall into a small windowless office. A tall man, middle-aged, dressed in an elegant suit, with carefully coiffed and oiled black hair, sat at the desk cleaning his nails with a tiny silver penknife. He stood up hurriedly as the door was opened and quickly hid the penknife in his trouser pocket. "Mr. Fox?" he asked.

"Yes," I said.

"Are you Mr. Alexander Fox?" he asked.

"I am," I said.

"I am Lieutenant Afgroni of the La Plata police. I am sorry to disturb you so early in the day, but I need to have a word with you. It was good of you to come so quickly."

"What for?" I asked. "What's this about?"

He looked over my shoulder at the clerk, who remained standing in the open door. "Thank you," he said to him. "If you would be so kind as to leave us alone." The clerk withdrew, closing the door behind him. Lieutenant Afgroni indicated a seat facing the desk, but I remained standing.

"I believe you are acquainted with a Mr. Richard Dent?" he asked. He pronounced Richard *Ree-shard.*

"Yes," I said. I knew it was the Dents. "I met him last evening."

"You were seen with him on the plaza late last night. Is that correct?"

"Yes," I said. "But what's this all about?"

"Mr. Dent is dead. His body was found in the harbor. I need you to identify it."

I sat down. "What happened?" I asked.

"Apparently he drowned. Presumably it was an accident. But we need a positive identification before we can proceed with the autopsy. As we are unable at the moment to locate Mrs. Dent, we have turned to you. The morgue is just across the plaza, in the municipal building. Will you accompany me?"

"I don't really know him," I said. "I just met him briefly last night. Hadn't you better wait for his wife?"

"I'm afraid we cannot. We regard this matter with some urgency." He opened the door. "It won't take long, I assure you, Mr. Fox. Will you come?"

I stood and followed him back through the lobby, across the plaza, and into the municipal building. A flight of marble steps ascended to a gallery, which ran around the perimeter of the entrance hall. Lieutenant Afgroni walked behind this staircase and opened a small unmarked door. "A shortcut," he announced. I followed him down a steep flight of stone steps into the basement. "This way," Lieutenant Afgroni said, and we turned down a long, brightly lit hallway. He stopped in front of a door marked MOR-TUAIRE. "Have you ever seen a drowned man before?" he asked me.

"I can't say I have," I said.

"It's not pretty," he said. "The body is a strange color, and there's a certain amount of bloat. And some ugly lacerations in this case as well. I don't want you to be shocked."

"I don't understand why you can't wait for Mrs. Dent. Don't you need a relative to identify a body?"

"No," he said, and opened the door. It was a small, cool room with two windows near the ceiling, at street level. The shadows of pigeons sulked against the frosted glass. In the center of the room was a high narrow table on which rested a body covered by a sheet. The sheet was bright yellow, which surprised me.

Lieutenant Afgroni stepped up to this table. "Are you ready?" he asked.

"Yes," I said. I stood beside him.

He peeled back the yellow sheet, revealing the face of the body. I laughed. I laughed because it was not Mr. Dent. Although there was a resemblance — a certain big-boned blondness — even allowing for discoloration and bloat, I knew that the obscene face on the absurd little pillow below me was not the face of Richard Dent.

"You laugh," said Lieutenant Afgroni.

"I laugh because I am relieved," I said. "It is not Mr. Dent. There is a certain likeness, but it is not Mr. Dent."

He covered the face with the sheet and then peeled it back, allowing us both another glimpse of the drowned man. This time he uncovered the neck as well, revealing a deep gash that ran vertically from below the ear to just above the collarbone. He looked at me. "You are sure this is not Mr. Dent?" he asked.

"Yes," I said.

"You seem very sure."

"I am," I said.

"Yet you told me you met him only last night."

"That is true."

"Then I wonder how you can be so sure. The face of a man is considerably altered by drowning. Perhaps Mr. Dent had some marks on his person — a mole, a tattoo. Are you aware of any such identifying marks on Mr. Dent's body?"

"I know of no such marks," I said. "This is a different man. I'm certain."

Lieutenant Afgroni reshrouded the face. "Thank you," he said. "Now if you would come with me, I would like to ask you a few questions."

"Is it really necessary? I've done what you asked me. I don't see how I can be of much help."

"Mr. Fox, assuming you are correct and this is not Mr. Dent, the fact remains that Mr. Dent has been reported suspiciously missing and you are quite possibly, as far as we know, the last person to see him. We hope you will be very helpful to us. Will you come with me?"

I nodded.

"Thank you," he said.

I followed him down the hall and into a small barren office, much like the office in the hotel. I felt as if I were seeing the backstage of Andorra, the small gray windowless rooms behind the fabulous scenery. "Please sit down," he said. "Would you like a coffee? Or a brandy?"

"May I have a brandy?" I asked.

"Of course," he said. "Do sit down."

I sat and Lieutenant Afgroni picked up a phone on the desk. "This is Afgroni," he said. "I'm in B4. Please bring us two brandies." He hung up the phone and sat down behind the desk. "Thank you for the help across the hall. I hope that wasn't too hard on you."

I was having trouble staying calm. I wanted time to stop so I could think, think about what to do and say. I wanted to be in my hotel room, in bed, or safe someplace in the sun.

A knock on the door. "*Entre*," said Lieutenant Afgroni. The door opened, revealing a young man in a tight-fitting police uniform which featured a ridiculous number of brass buttons. For a moment I mistook him for the valet at the hotel, so similar was his uniform. He carried a small tray on which stood two glasses and a bottle of brandy. "On the desk, please, Edward," said Lieutenant Afgroni.

The young man lowered the tray onto the desk. "Will you excuse me for one moment, Mr. Fox?" asked Lieutenant Afgroni.

"Yes," I said.

The two men went into the hall and closed the door. I could hear them talking, but I couldn't make out what they were saying. I looked at my watch: it was only 9:00. I poured some brandy into a glass and drank it. The door opened and Lieutenant Afgroni reseated himself behind the desk. He picked up the bottle of brandy and, seeing the amber sheen in one of the glasses, said, "I see that you helped yourself."

"Yes," I said. "I did."

"Would you like another?"

"Please," I said.

He poured two brandies, and handed one to me. He held the other in his hand. "Please relax, Mr. Fox, if you can. I'm sorry to have to detain you like this, but as you were one of the last people to see Mr. Dent, I'm sure you'll understand why it's imperative that we speak with you."

"Yes," I said. "I understand."

"Good," he said. "You had dinner with the Dents last night?"

"Yes," I said.

"Where?"

"At their house."

"Ah," he said, "I see. And then Mr. Dent walked you back to the hotel?"

"Yes," I said.

"What time was that?"

"I'm not sure, exactly. Late."

"Can you be more exact?"

I thought for a moment, and then I remembered the fountain lights extinguishing and looking at my watch. "It was midnight," I said. "I remember because the fountain went off."

"Of course," he said. "Midnight." He made a note of this. "Was Mr. Dent . . . had he been drinking?"

"Some," I said. "But he did not seem inebriated."

"I presume that you, too, had been drinking."

"No more than Mr. Dent. Some wine with dinner, and then some brandy."

"Exactly," said Lieutenant Afgroni. "Mr. Dent accompanied you to your room, did he not?"

"He did," I said.

"And what was the purpose of his visit?"

"I invited him up for a nightcap."

"I see," said Lieutenant Afgroni. "And then what happened?"

"We had a drink and talked for a while, and then he left."

"Was it your understanding he was returning home?"

"Yes," I said. "I supposed. He had his dog with him."

"A dog?"

"Yes. A very large dog. Called Dino."

"Dino?"

"Yes."

Lieutenant Afgroni also noted this: MIDNIGHT, DINO. "And you say you went to bed then and never saw Mr. Dent again."

"Yes. Well, actually, I did see him again."

"You did? Where?"

"Before going to bed, I stepped out on my balcony. I saw Mr. Dent sitting on the fountain. On the rim of the fountain."

"And that was the last you saw of him?"

"Yes. That was the last I saw of him."

"Very well," said Lieutenant Afgroni. "May I ask you how long you have known the Dents?"

"I met Mr. Dent last night. I've known Mrs. Dent only a few days. Since my arrival in Andorra."

"And when was that?"

"I arrived on Monday."

"Monday the seventeenth of May?"

"That is correct."

"May I ask at what time?"

"In the morning. I took the overnight train from Paris."

"Of course," said Lieutenant Afgroni. "I know it well. And you said you met Mrs. Dent that very same day?"

"That is correct," I said.

"You did not know her prior to your arrival here?"

"I told you, I met her on Monday."

"So you did. I'm sorry to appear rude. But while I am trespassing upon your wonderful tolerance I would like to ask you one more question, if I may. It goes back to the identification of the body across the hall. I assure you this question presupposes nothing. Do you happen to know if Mr. Dent was circumcised?"

"I have not the least idea," I said.

"I thought as much. I see I have insulted you. Forgive me. I have inconvenienced you enough for one day, Mr. Fox. The La Plata Municipal Police Squadron thanks you, as do I." He stood up. "I thank you very much. Let me show you out." He opened the door and I followed him down the hall and up the staircase into the entry hall. I was very glad to see the world outside its doors. "I assume your passport is at the hotel?" Lieutenant Afgroni asked.

"It is," I said.

"And you are an American citizen?"

"I am," I said.

"We may need to keep it here for a day or two. Would that inconvenience you?"

"Why do you need my passport?" I asked.

"Merely a formality. Were you planning to leave the country in the near future?"

"No," I said. "I was planning to stay in Andorra for quite some time."

"Good. Then it wouldn't inconvenience you to leave your passport with us?"

"No," I said.

"Fine, then. I'll send Edward for it. You might tell them at the hotel he'll be coming. I can't thank you enough, Mr. Fox. You've been extraordinarily patient and helpful." He extended his manicured hand. I shook it, and then walked out onto the sunlit plaza.

1 STOOD ON THE PLAZA FOR A MOMENT TRYING TO DECIDE
where to go, trying not to look as if I was deciding where to go. I
had the feeling Lieutenant Afgroni was watching me from inside
the building, but I did not want to turn around and look. I wished
I smoked, so that I could light a cigarette. I patted my pockets as
if I were looking for one. And then I walked toward, and into, the
tobacconist, which was one of the few stores on the plaza I had not
yet explored. It was a cool, dark shop filled with the pungent odor
of tobacco. Shanks of it hung from the ceiling, and dried bits of it
crumbled to powder on the floor. Large glass and ceramic urns of
different tobaccos stood on a counter.

"May I help you?" asked a young woman standing behind the
counter. She wore a white laboratory coat, as if she were a scientist.
I have always abhorred that sort of shameless sartorial misrepresen-
tation: makeup girls idling around cosmetic counters disguised as
nuclear physicists. It blurs the sharp focus of the world.

"No, thank you," I said. I turned around and walked out. I felt
a sort of weird anger and rage short-circuiting inside me; I tried to
convince myself it was a result of my visit to the masquerading
tobacconist, but I knew it was not. I needed to sit somewhere and
calm down and think. I didn't want to go to the cantina and I did

not want to return to the hotel. I wanted to get away someplace quiet and private and dark. I began to walk up a narrow street that led from the plaza to the second terrace, and then climbed a flight of steps to the third terrace. I turned up a busy street of shops, looking for a café into which I might disappear, and suddenly found myself in front of the coffee store below Uncle Roderick's apartment. I looked inside. The coffee bar in the front of the store was filled with men smoking and reading newspapers and drinking little cups of espresso. There was something native and comradely about their company that seemed to exclude foreigners. And I was, after all, a foreigner. I stood on the street for a moment, wondering what to do. I felt defeated, an outcast, and then I remembered the little iron key beneath the pot of desiccated geraniums, and the empty quiet apartment right above me. I walked quickly and purposefully into the covered alley, hoping that no one had seen me. The little courtyard was deserted and the garbage had been removed; I assumed Miss Quay had spoken with Ali about it. I hurried up the steps and squatted outside the door, reached beneath the pot, and felt for the key. It was there. I unlocked the door and stepped inside, closing the door behind me.

It was only then that I realized I was panting and sweating. I stood just inside the closed door for a while and tried to regain some sense of calm. I closed my eyes and stood with my back against the door, and allowed whatever it was coursing through my body to exhaust itself. Then I opened my eyes.

It was dark and quiet in the apartment. The drapes were drawn across the large windows, and I tried to remember if we had closed them before we left. Or had someone been in the apartment since

then? But there was obviously no one in here now: it was all still-
ness and silence. I laid the key on a table inside the door and
walked to the center of the dark room. I lay down on the floor and
looked up at the beamed ceiling. Where was Mrs. Dent? If she had
reported Mr. Dent missing, why was she not at the police's disposal?
That seemed very strange. Perhaps she had gone out looking for
Mr. Dent. As if he were a cat, or a dog. Calling Ricky! Ricky!
through the streets. What's Ricky short for when it's a woman? Was
she Ricky before she married Mr. Dent, or did she become Ricky
then? I don't know. It would be awkward to ask her that now. I
closed my eyes, so it was completely dark. The two brandies I had
drunk began to take effect, and I saw the veldt again, my dark veldt
with the phosphorizing sky above it.

As I pushed myself through the revolving door of the Hotel Excelsior, I saw Mrs. Dent standing in the center of the lobby. The carpet
had an intricate design that erupted outward in an ever-widening
and more complex pattern of garlands from a medallion at its center, and it was on this medallion that Mrs. Dent frozenly stood, as
if a director had given her a mark and forbidden her to move. She
watched me cross the lobby. "Have you heard," she asked me in a
strange, low voice, "Ricky's disappeared?"

"Yes, I've heard. I've almost been arrested, in fact. My passport's
been confiscated and I've been identifying drowned bodies all
morning."

"Isn't it awful?" she said. "I just saw it. But thank God it's not
Ricky."

"What's going on?" I asked. "Where have you been?"

"I went out to Crowespoint," she said.

"Crowespoint?"

"The beach club. I thought he might have gotten it in his head to go out there for a swim last night, after our conversation. I've been looking all over for him."

"Why did you call the police? And why did you set them on me? It's only been a couple of hours."

"I heard they'd found another body. Of course I was upset. I'm sorry. But he's not with you?"

"No," I said. "Why would he be with me?"

"I don't—I just thought—God! Did he say he was coming home? What time did you leave him?"

"He left me," I said, "about midnight." I could tell she was genuinely alarmed. Her face was pale and there was something clenched and desperate about her.

"Why don't you sit down," I told her, and we sat next to one another on a divan.

"Where did he leave you?" she asked.

"He came up to my room for a drink. We talked for a while, and then he left."

"I don't know where he could be," she said. "Dino came back about three, dragging his leash, barking. He woke me up. I've been up ever since then, waiting."

"He's probably home now," I said. "Perhaps you should go back."

"No," she said. "If everything was all right, he would have kept Dino with him. I know that something's wrong."

"Has this ever happened before?"

"No," she said. "Not since — not since we moved here. In Sydney, yes. But not here."

"Well, I'm sure he's just stayed out walking. Or whatever."

"Did you upset him?"

I realized I was a little afraid of her. She clutched the edge of the cushion and stared at me, her face wide and almost ugly with alarm.

"No," I said. "I did not upset him."

"What did you talk about?"

"Oh, I don't remember. Nothing particularly memorable or upsetting. Anyway, I'm sure he's arrived home while you've been out. He's probably worried about you."

I stood, but Mrs. Dent remained seated. "I need to get some coffee and breakfast," I said. "I've had nothing to eat all morning. I'd ask you to join me, but I really think you should go home."

She wasn't looking at me. She was looking down into her lap, and suddenly she collapsed forward and began to weep, covering her face with her hands. I sat back beside her. I didn't know what to say or do. She was weeping strongly yet quietly, and that made it worse somehow, the struggling quiet of it. I put my hand on Mrs. Dent's shoulder and held it there until she stopped crying. She raised her head a little and wiped at her wet eyes with her hands. "Could we go someplace less public?" she asked.

As I did not want to take her to my room, I thought immediately of the library, which I was sure would be deserted at that time of day. I stood up and so did she. One or two people lowered the leaves of their newspaper and stared curiously and censoriously at us. I wanted to spit at them. We walked across the lobby and up the staircase to the first floor and down the hall. The glass doors to the library were closed and the room was dark; I hadn't noticed before that it had no windows. I opened the doors and looked about for the switch to light the chandelier that hung over the large reading table at the center of the room. But I could find no switch. I remembered the small lamps on the shelves that stayed lit for a moment or two with a press of a button, and walked across the room into one of the bays and felt for the button. The light went on. I was in Continental Fiction. Mrs. Dent had remained in the hall. "Come here," I said. "Close the door."

She entered the room, closed the door behind her, and then walked through the darkness and stood beside me in the little pool of light. "I'm sorry about that, down there," she said. "I hope I didn't embarrass you."

"Of course not," I said, although she had.

"Sometimes it's hell being married," she said. She tipped a book out from a shelf and then nudged it back in without really looking at it. "This happened often in Sydney: Ricky disappearing, I mean. But it hasn't happened once in the years we've been here. I can't bear it if it all starts again."

"Where does he go?" I asked.

"He won't say. Of course I know he's with men, but he won't ever admit it. He's terribly ashamed of what he does."

"And you thought he was with me last night?"

"Well, yes. I mean, it made sense. You did walk off together into the night."

"I'm not homosexual," I said.

She looked at me. "Neither is Ricky," she said.

I supposed she meant he was bisexual, or some such nonsense. "To a certain extent, you're right," I said. "He did try to seduce me. But nothing came of it. He had a drink and left, as I told you. Perhaps he's home by now. With his tail between his legs."

"Don't patronize him," she said.

"I'm sorry," I said. "I wasn't."

"Of course you were. It's small of you. And mean. I didn't think you were like that."

"It's only that to see you like this—so upset—it makes me angry at him."

"Were you cruel to him?"

"What do you mean?"

"Last night. Were you cruel to him?"

"No," I said. "Of course I wasn't."

"Good," she said. "Thank you for that. I know you must think our marriage is some pathetic sham, but it isn't. It's a real and proper marriage, and I love Ricky with all my soul. Despite all this. You probably can't understand that, but it's true."

I didn't say anything. The light went out, and we were in darkness, just a vague glow coming in from the hallway.

"I'd better go home," Mrs. Dent said, "so I'm there when Ricky gets back."

"Yes," I said.

"I'm sorry if you feel dragged into our mess," she said. "I expect you'll want nothing to do with us from now on."

"Of course not," I said, although I was glad she was leaving.

She smiled at me, and we began to walk toward the door. She

said, "There's no need for you to come downstairs with me. I've ruined enough of your day."

"Not at all," I said. We walked down the hall and paused at the top of the stairs. "Listen: will you let me know that Ricky's safe?" I asked.

"Yes," she said. She reached out and touched her hand to my cheek, held it there for a moment, and then hurried down the stairs and across the lobby and out the revolving doors.

I went up to my room and took off my clothes, which stank of sweat and cologne. I showered and dressed. I was hungry and thought about having a late breakfast in the safety of my room, but I thought, No, you must go back down there. And I did. I had a pleasant meal in a sunny corner of the courtyard. I sat there in that perfect place, the silver warm in my grip, the butter softening in its ramekin, the only sound the occasional splash of a fish penetrating the surface of its fountain world. Here I am, I thought, having breakfast in the garden of the Hotel Excelsior!

I sliced the yolk of my single poached egg so that it rained its molten gold over the toast.

Later that afternoon I met with Edward Darlingham, the Quays' solicitor, and arranged to rent Roderick Wynstan Quay's apartment at No. 16 San Julián de Loria for six months, with an option to renew for a like period of time. I could move in as soon as I wished.

That evening a note from Mrs. Dent arrived. It completes this episode.

All's well that ends well? Much ado about nothing? Well, let's hope. You were right: Ricky was back here waiting for me, after wandering the streets all night. Poor darling! We're sailing off to Ibiza for a couple of days, to relax and be together, but will see you when we return. I can't thank you enough for holding my hand, literally and figuratively, in my most desperate and neurotic moments. You're a real friend, and we both send our best love —

PART TWO

NO. 16 SAN JULIÁN DE LORIA

Seldom, very seldom, does com-
plete truth belong to any human
disclosure; seldom can it happen
that something is not a little dis-
guised, or a little mistaken.

—JANE AUSTEN, *Emma*

*M*RS. DENT HAD BEEN RIGHT: MY ROOM AT THE EXCELSIOR WAS a place of God, and I was sorry to leave it. After the valet had packed my trunk and carted it down the spiral steps (the hotel was arranging its transportation to Uncle Roderick's) I stood alone for a few minutes, thinking about all that had happened to me in the week I had lived here. I stepped out on the balcony and looked for one last time at the view that had briefly been mine, and never again would be. Thousands of people had possessed this view, but that made it no less mine.

Whenever I think of Andorra, I will see it first as I first really saw it: spread out below me, sun-struck, wonderful.

I left all the doors and windows open. It was a fine day, and a warm wind blew through the room, bearing the last traces of me from it.

My trunk had been left in the living room and I managed to push it up the interior staircase into the bedroom. Some of Uncle Roderick's suits still inhabited the closet, hanging along the pole at regular intervals, so that none touched another. He was a large man by the look of them—a large man partial to tweed and waistcoats. With a stiffened arm I raked them all to one side and hung my own clothes in the vacated space, leaving a gap between his clothes and mine.

And I did the same sort of thing throughout the house: inserting my life, my meager belongings, alongside Uncle Roderick's many, and then I set about figuring out how my life in Andorra was to be lived on a daily basis. In those first few days I arrived at the following schedule: I awoke in the morning to the almost overpowering smell of coffee rising from Ali's store two floors below me. After a quick shower I'd go downstairs and have a cup or two of espresso with all the men crowded into the café in the front of the store. From there it was a short walk to the market, where I would buy a waxed paper cone filled with freshly made yoghurt and whatever fruit looked especially appetizing. These I would eat sitting outside on my terrace, where I would spend most of the morning writing in my journal or reading. By noon it would be too hot to remain outdoors and I would come inside and read for a while longer, and then have something cold to drink, before venturing down to the cantina for lunch. I ate inside or out, depending on the weather and the availability of tables. After lunch I would come back home and take a nap, arising an hour or two later as the afternoon waned, and spend the last hours of it exploring some new part of town.

I discovered the beach club one afternoon: a house called Crowespoint, very much like Quayside, at the tip of the peninsula. There was a genteel yet faded restaurant and lounge on the ground floor, but the remainder of the building had been converted into a convalescent/geriatric center. The stables had been transformed into men's and women's changing rooms, and from there one descended a flight of small stone steps inscribed into the steep cliff.

The sandy beach was often crowded, but the water was sublime: cool and clear and the most lovely turquoise color imaginable. After swimming I often had a drink on the terrace of the house, and although people nodded and smiled at me, no one approached or seemed approachable. I realized how lucky I had been to meet Mrs. Dent, and that I missed her.

I returned to the hotel for dinner one evening, and found Mrs. Reinhardt in the library afterwards and read her the first chapter of *A Sentimental Journey*. If there was something interesting on at the theater or the opera, I attended, but I rationed these evenings, as their repertories were small and I believed my nights were to be many.

One morning it rained, and I found this change in weather agitating. I stood in the living room and watched the rain fall out on the terrace, puddling up on the mosaic table and dripping off its edges onto the stone floor. I tried to settle down on the couch with some books and my journal, but I couldn't concentrate. Although it was still raining hard, I decided I needed some fresh air, exercise, a change of place: a walk. In arranging the closet I had noticed a particularly impermeable-looking raincoat of Uncle Roderick's, and I decided to wear that instead of my own, which, though British and elegant, was surprisingly and disappointingly inefficient in repelling moisture. I had taken to wearing some of Uncle Roddy's things about the house, in fact. I had found a beautifully embroidered gauze nightshirt that suited the decor of the bed too perfectly for me not to wear it, and some interesting French undershorts that, though too large, could be cinched in at the waist with little silver buckles. The raincoat was, however, the first garment of his that I had worn in public.

But there was very little public about: the town was deserted. I had the feeling Andorrans were fairly unaccustomed to rain and simply avoided it, which made perfect sense, as the storms never seemed to last very long. I walked through the market; the rain-washed fruits and vegetables looked particularly fresh and flavorful, but the other wares were shrouded with sheets of clear plastic, and the merchants sat beneath leaking canopies or dripping umbrellas, looking glum. The plaza was empty. I decided to venture out to the beach club and have a look at the sea in the rain. I noticed as I passed that the gates of Quayside were shut, and though I peered through them, I could see nothing but wet privet. I continued walking to the end of the peninsula road and then up the gravel drive of Crowespoint. I wandered through the clubhouse, but there was no one about: just a gaggle of waitresses loitering outside the kitchen door, and one table of women, smoking and talking over coffee, pastries, and heaping ashtrays. I stepped out on the terrace and looked down at the sea. Its own internal motion seemed to be stilled by that of the rain; it looked abnormally placid, and I could actually see the thousands of little pinpricks the rain was making on its surface, battening it down, sewing it to the surface of the earth. I decided to go down to the beach for a closer look. The stairs were wet and slippery and I held on tightly to the pipe-like railing that was set into the rock, but it shook in my grasp, and I knew that if I slipped I might go hurtling over the edge.

No one was on the beach. It felt warmer down there, secluded, and the rain seemed to have abated a little. I walked a way along the sand and then took off my shoes and socks and rolled up my pants legs and stood in the surf, although it wasn't really surf: just a gentle, apathetic unfurling. The water felt much warmer than it looked, and I tried to pull my pants farther up my legs, but they bunched around my calves.

I wanted to be in the water.

At the end of the public beach a pile of huge rocks extended from the base of the cliff out into the sea, bisecting the beach, and I thought that if I climbed over this wall I could perhaps swim privately on the opposite side. As I approached it I saw that a sign guaranteed this. It read: PRIVATE BEACHES BEYOND THIS POINT. NO TRESPASSING. I climbed over the rocks, which were slick with seaweed and rainwater and studded with small black snails. I pulled a shell off the rocks and watched the snail retract itself, curling its moist plump body into its little cave, sealing itself with its tiny enameled door. I envied its ability to be self-contained, intact. To have as part of one's anatomy both a shell and an unlockable door. I tossed it into the water, watching for the little splash it made.

The seawall was taller than it looked from a distance, but I got over it without mishap. I discovered myself in a small, still cove, bounded by the seawall on one side and an indentation in the cliff on the others. I quickly removed my clothes, folding them carefully inside Uncle Roderick's raincoat, and lowered myself from a rock into the water. For a moment I just let it embrace me, moving only so much as to stay afloat. And then I sank down into it, exhaling all of my breath, falling as my breath unblossomed above me in a hurtling trail of bubbles. The farther down I sank, the colder and darker the water grew, and when I realized I would not touch the bottom I panicked and clawed and kicked myself back up through it, sputtering a bit as I reemerged. It was raining harder now — that final burst of rain that comes at a storm's end — and the sweetness of the rainwater combined itself with the salt of the sea, creating an effervescent world at its surface that I floated happily in for a few minutes. I closed my eyes and let the rain pelt my face.

Presently I heard through the water a different, more regular rhythm than that of the rain. SPLASH-splash, SPLASH-splash, SPLASH-splash. I opened my eyes and raised my head a little and looked around me. About thirty feet away was a kayak, in which no other than Mrs. Quay was ensconced. She was wearing a green sou'wester and a matching hat, and had pulled the paddle from the water and rested it across the top of her boat, so that it dripped a steady stream from either flattened end. She put a hand up over her eyes as if she was shielding them from the sun and said, "You are either Mr. Fox or a merman. I can't tell which from here and I daren't come any closer lest you are a merman and I am lured to my death."

"Good morning, Mrs. Quay," I said.

"Mr. Fox, I presume?"

"Yes," I said. "I walked down to the beach and couldn't resist a swim in the rain."

"Au naturel by the looks of it," said Mrs. Quay.

I glanced down, and for once cursed the water's lucidity. "Excuse me," I said. "I thought I would be alone."

"And so you would be, if it weren't for crazy old kayaking ladies like me. But don't be embarrassed, Mr. Fox; on the contrary, be proud! I should like to kayak au naturel but don't have the gumption. Although I must admit that on particularly sunny days when

I achieve a safe distance from the shore I remove my blouse. You see, I am not as matronly as you think."

"I never thought you matronly," I said.

"You are charming to lie. And much as I would like to stay and chat with you, I hardly feel this is the time or the place. Will you come have lunch with us on your way back to town? As this is a peninsula and you are in the water at its tip, you can't say it's not on your way."

"I would like to very much," I said. "Thank you."

She looked up at the sky. "I think the sun will be out by then," she said. She inserted her paddle into the water and pulled it, deftly turning the kayak away from me, and SPLASH-splash, SPLASH-splash, SPLASH-splash: she was gone.

As I approached Quayside the sun did appear, at first glimmering and then bursting through the clouds as it had on my previous visit, and I felt I would always encounter it thus: rinsed clean by rain and sparkling in the sun, like some little trinket lifted from the ocean and set, still dripping, on the cliff.

I was glad the sun had come out, for I was a little anxious about arriving at Quayside in Uncle Roderick's raincoat—it was distinctive enough to be recognized, and I was sure the Quays would disapprove of me borrowing my landlord's clothes. But the change in weather allowed me to remove the coat, which I carefully folded and stowed beneath a huge rhododendron bush just inside the gate. A rabbit had made her nest beneath the bush, a sunken hollow upholstered with leaves and fur in which five baby rabbits mewled. I squatted for a moment on the damp grass and watched them.

They looked like rodent offspring; there was really nothing to suggest rabbit about them yet. I envied them a little: to be born on the lawn at Quayside and to live out their lives on that sunny, indolent slope.

I looked at my watch before I rang the bell. It was a few minutes past one. It was some time before the door was opened. Miss Quay stood inside, panting a little. "Oh—" she said. "Mr. Fox."

"Hello," I said.

"Yes," she said. "Hello. What brings you here?"

"Your mother invited me for lunch," I said. "I met her near Crowespoint. I was swimming, and she was kayaking."

"How active you both are. Well, you have returned before her. But please come in. Have you no coat?"

"No," I said. "The weather is quite fine now."

She looked out the door before closing it. "It is," she said. "I've been upstairs with Bitsy all morning. She's in bed with an earache. I don't suppose you'd like to visit a four-year-old invalid? Bitsy is my niece."

"Yes," I said. "You told me all about her."

"That's right," said Miss Quay. "That first evening—" She must have remembered our kiss, for she looked down at the slate floor.

"I would very much like to meet her," I said.

Miss Quay looked at me, but said nothing. She nodded at the stairs, and started to climb them. I followed her up one flight and then down a long, dark hallway across whose narrow space ancestral portraits peered disdainfully at one another. Then we went up another staircase. I walked quite closely behind Miss Quay, who climbed the steps carefully and rigidly, her spine perfectly straight, so that her body barely touched her shiftlike dress. She climbed the stairs as if it were bad manners to have a body. I had a sudden wild urge—I suppose urges are always wild—to lean forward and bite her invisible, but implied, rump.

The staircase turned several corners, up, up, up, but Miss Quay did not once look over her shoulder. Then a long hall with flowered wallpaper instead of paintings, and into a large room that was obviously the nursery, with a play area, a fireplace, a kitchenette with a child-size dining table, and a sleeping alcove which contained a little canopied bed. A dollhouse-sized replica of Quayside sat on the floor in the play area. A young girl in a white nightgown, her dark hair in two braids, squatted expectantly on top of the bed.

"I told you to stay beneath the covers," said Miss Quay.

"Who was it?" asked the girl.

"It was Mr. Fox," said Miss Quay, "and he's come to say hello to you, but you must get under the blankets, otherwise he'll go away."

The girl did this. Miss Quay sat down beside her and tucked the bedclothes snugly around her. How wonderful it is to tuck someone, or be tucked, into bed. Miss Quay laid one of her hands on the girl's forehead. I stood beside the bed. She looked nothing like my daughter, but something about her pose on top of the bed— that way children who have been left behind eagerly await the return of a beloved adult: poised and tense with gleeful affection— well, I had discovered Anna in that same position night after night, as I came into her room to say good night and to tell or read to her a story.

"Mr. Fox—" I heard Miss Quay say, but I couldn't really focus on her. I was looking at the white quilted duvet, trying to fill up my eyes, my head, with its wonderful annihilating whiteness. I heard Miss Quay get up from the bed and I felt her put her hand on my shoulder. "Are you all right?" she asked. I thought about the grace of her hand; how she had delicately palmed her niece's forehead, touched my shoulder; how her hand would continue its gentle and benevolent course through life. I wanted to kiss it or put it in the Museum of Astounding Body Parts or exhibit it in a reliquary with the ashen bones of saints. I felt Miss Quay leading me out of the room and down the flowered hall into a tiny bedroom next door to the nursery, where she seated me in a rocking chair and sat herself on the bed opposite me. She leaned her face close to mine and asked me again if I was all right.

Sitting down helped me reinhabit myself, and after a moment I looked at her and said yes.

"Do you feel ill?" she asked. "You're quite pale."

"No," I said. "Seeing your niece. It reminded me of—"

She did not press me. "Why don't you sit here for a moment? Let me go check on Bitsy. I think you gave her a fright. Would you like something to drink? A glass of water?"

"Yes, thank you," I said.

She leaned forward once again and took one of my hands in both of hers. I wanted to collapse forward and be held by her, but I knew I should not. I could not remember the last time I had been held by anyone.

She returned my hand and stood. "I'll be right back," she said, and left me alone. After a moment I rose and looked around the room. I realized it must be the governess's bedroom, although it appeared uninhabited: just a Bible on the night table and a vase of dusty dried flowers on the bureau. I looked out the window and saw Mrs. Quay coming up the path from the beach.

"Who are you?" I heard a voice ask. I turned away from the window and saw a woman standing in the door. She was younger than Miss Quay but just as tall, and more beautiful in a sultry, disheveled fashion. With one hand she held the lapels of her dragony kimono closed tightly at her throat; in the other hand she held a cigarette. Her hair was rather a mess and her face had the look of needing a wash, or makeup, or some other enlivening and organizing attention.

"I am Alexander Fox," I said.

"I should have known," she said. "You're the new man renting Uncle Roddy's flat, aren't you?"

"Yes," I said.

"I'm delighted to meet you. I am Nancy. Nancy Quay Flyte Bottom, to be precise and exhaustive. I'm thinking of dropping the Bottom, though, and just going as Nancy Quay Flyte. Sounds rather like an Indian princess, I think." She removed her hand from her throat and held it out in my direction. I could not help noticing that she had been right to clutch her kimono close; it now gaped open, revealing the beautiful yet alarming topography of her décolletage.

I shook it (her hand) and said, "It's nice to meet you."

"I'm sure it can't be, looking as I do. But what on earth are you doing up here in Nanny's old bedroom? Are you hiding out?"

"No," I said, but before I could explain, Mrs. Quay appeared in the doorway.

"Nancy, I've told you a thousand times not to smoke near the nursery. Especially when Bitsy isn't well. Mr. Fox, please excuse my not being here to greet you. The tide was against me. Or at least I chose to think it was. Perhaps you would like to come downstairs and have a drink?"

"Certainly," I said.

"I could use a drink," said Nancy.

"It looks as if you could better use a bath and change of clothes," said Mrs. Quay. She turned and left the room, waiting for me in the hallway. As I passed by Nancy I heard her whisper, just loud enough so I could hear, "Stupid old bitch."

We did not eat in the dining room but on a round table set up in a small sitting room off the main hall. Nancy Quay Flyte (Bottom?) reappeared about halfway through lunch. She had obviously taken her mother's suggestion to heart, for she was washed and costumed. With her hair elegantly arranged on her head, and dressed in a tailored suit with a longish skirt and a tight bolero jacket, she looked quite a different woman.

"You're dressed oddly for luncheon" was how her mother greeted her.

"I'm just trying to repair my image with Mr. Fox," said Nancy. She sat down between Mrs. Quay and me. "Although perhaps it's futile. Mr. Fox, do you think first impressions are intractable?"

"You mean retractable," said Miss Quay, "or at least something more like that."

"Mr. Fox knows what I mean," said Nancy.

I attempted to change the course of the conversation by asking if the Quays performed any civil services.

"Of course we do," said Mrs. Quay. "It is a program initiated by my late husband, so it would be unthinkable for us not to participate."

"And what do you do?" I asked.

"I am the Director of the Girl Guides. And in addition to that, I write and produce the historical pageant that is performed every year on St. Umiliana's Day. She is the patron saint of our country. We are working our way through Andorran history from the ice ages to the present. This year finds us in the early nineteenth century. Perhaps I can write you a part in the pageant this year, Mr. Fox. Do you sing?"

"I am afraid I don't," I said.

"What a shame. I like a man who sings. It is an admirable quality in a man."

"And not a woman?"

"For some reason there is always something unexpected about a man who sings. Something delightful and surprising. One supposes women can sing. Or at least I do. Although I don't know why, since I have a voice like a frog. Jean has a lovely voice. She got it from her father."

"I can sing," said Nancy.

"You can," said Mrs. Quay, "but not as well as Jean. It is a fact, not an opinion, my dear."

"When is the pageant?" I asked.

"It is traditionally the penultimate Sunday in October. I am glad you have reminded me of it, for it is time to start planning. And I am glad to know you have been considering the civil service. From whom did you learn of it?"

"My friends the Dents mentioned it to me. They suggested I might work at the Biblioteca."

"The Dents? I don't believe I know the Dents. Who are the Dents?"

"They are a couple from Australia. They've been living here for a year or two, on the fourth terrace. I met them quite by accident."

"That is no way to make friends," said Mrs. Quay. "And the fourth terrace is hardly the place one would go seeking one's society."

"Mother," said Jean, "you sound an awful snob. We know many people who live on the fourth. And besides, where someone lives has no bearing on their character."

"Yet it is indicative of something," said Mrs. Quay. "I'm sure the Dents are lovely people, if Mr. Fox is associated with them. I just wouldn't want him falling in with the wrong set, that is all."

"I suppose you mean my friends," said Nancy.

"I don't think Mr. Fox would have any interest in your friends, Nancy," said Mrs. Quay.

"And I think you have a lot of nerve deciding what sort of friends are right for Mr. Fox. I'm sure he can decide without your help, Mother."

"You misunderstand me. I am not deciding for him; I am giving him information so that he can decide for himself. He does not know the lay of the societal land, so to speak."

"Your ideas are hopelessly archaic," said Nancy.

"I'm sure you think they are, my dear. Now, why don't you go up and check on your invalid daughter?"

"I checked on her before I came down. She's sleeping."

"I'll check on her," said Miss Quay. She stood up and placed her napkin on her chair.

Mrs. Quay watched Jean leave the room, and when she turned back to the table she had nothing to say.

"She was sleeping," Nancy repeated, after a moment. "I'm sure she still is."

"Nevertheless," said Mrs. Quay, "one likes to check."

Nancy poured herself a glass of wine. She drank from it, and then used her napkin to wipe off the kiss her lipstick had left on its rim.

We sat for a moment in awkward silence, and then, in an effort to restart the conversation, I asked Nancy where she did her civil service.

"I don't," she said, a little brusquely. "I don't believe in enforced philanthropy. It seems rather a contradiction in terms."

"It's not enforced," said Mrs. Quay. "You know perfectly well that it's voluntary."

"Everyone pretends it is, but it isn't. I get a notice every month."

"Simply a reminder," said Mrs. Quay. "In case you change your mind."

Nancy laughed darkly and unhappily, and then turned to me. "I take it you're thinking of working at the dreaded Biblioteca?" she asked.

"Yes," I said.

"I can't stand books," Nancy said with sudden bitterness, as if books were to blame for everything that had gone wrong in her life. "I know it only confirms what a dunce I am, but it's the truth." She sipped again at her wine and then brushed nothing vehemently from the lap of her skirt. "Even the smell of them makes me physically ill," she added.

"More pudding, Mr. Fox?" asked Mrs. Quay.

"No, thank you," I said.

"What about coffee? Or perhaps a pastis? We could have it on the loggia, I think. I'm sure it's dry enough by now."

"Actually," I said, "I should be returning home. I hadn't meant to stay away this long."

"I suppose we have detained you. But it was a pleasure. Won't you go upstairs and say goodbye to Jean before you leave? You can find your way up to the nursery, I trust?"

"I can," I said. "And shall."

"In that case I will say goodbye now. It is time for my nap. I'm so glad I ran into you, such as it was, and that you could join us for lunch. I know we shall see you again soon, and I look forward to it."

I stood up and followed Mrs. Quay to the door, where I shook her hand, thanked her, and bid her goodbye.

Nancy loitered at the table.

"It was nice to meet you," I said to her from the doorway.

"Would you like a cigarette?" she asked me.

"No, thank you," I said.

"Will you keep me company while I smoke?" she asked.

"Of course," I said, and reseated myself.

She took a cigarette from a marcasite box on the sideboard and lit it. She sat down and poured the last inch of wine from the bottle into my glass. "So," she said, "you know the Dents?"

"Yes," I said. "Do you know them?"

"Not really. I mean, one sees her around, with that dog. He's quite a good-looking man, I think. You say they're Austrian?"

"Australian," I said.

"Yes, of course. Australian. Are you Australian?"

"I'm an American," I said.

"Are you? You don't seem one."

"What do I seem?" I asked.

She looked at me, and flicked her ashes into her half-finished bowl of pudding. "I don't know. There's something odd about you I can't put my finger on. And I should so like to put my finger on it. Do you have other friends here, besides the Dents?"

"Not really," I said. "Part of the reason I've come here is to be alone."

"I hate to be alone," said Nancy. "I suppose that's because I don't really like myself. How different we are. You must like yourself very much. Do you?"

"I am trying to," I said.

"And are you succeeding?"

"It's too early to tell," I said.

"Well, I wish you all the luck in the world, although I don't see why it should be so difficult. If I were you, I would like you. Would you like me if you were me?"

"I think you should like yourself," I said.

"Why?" she asked.

"Because it is a good thing. A healthy thing."

"No, you misunderstand. I mean specifically. Why should I like myself? What are the reasons for me liking myself?"

"You must find your own reasons," I said. "Only they will have meaning."

"How tactful you are. When I was little I used to think tactful meant full of tacks. I still do, in a way." She put her cigarette out and stood up. "I suppose I should go check on my daughter. It is something one does here, as you have no doubt noticed. We are forever checking on Bitsy."

"She's a lovely little girl," I said. "I hope she is feeling better."

"Oh, please," said Nancy. "She's a small girl with a little earache. I am sure she will outlive us all."

CHAPTER ELEVEN

My visit to quayside left me slightly discomfited, and I decided to take off for a day or two and explore the Vega, the only part of the country I had yet to see.

In order to find out how best to get there and where to stay and what to see once there—those elemental questions of travel—I went down to the coffee store to talk to Ali. We had struck up a cordial relationship: we exchanged greetings when I joined the throng for my morning coffee, and sometimes in the afternoon, when I stopped on my way home from a walk for an oily and rejuvenating espresso, he would sit down and talk with me. Doris, his wife, who seemed to be constantly sweeping or mopping the marble floor, never spoke. I had the feeling her silence was elected, but I wasn't sure.

When I entered the store it was empty, as it often was in the early afternoon, and Ali was sitting at one of the little café tables, smoking a hand-rolled cigarette. "And how are you this very hot afternoon?" he asked me.

"I'm fine," I said.

"And what could I get you?"

"I would like an espresso," I said.

"It will be yours," he said, and stood up. I sat looking out the window at the empty street, and heard the hiss of the espresso maker from behind me. Ali returned with the little ceramic cup and placed it in front of me. He sat down.

"Actually," I said, "I'm thinking of going away for a day or two."

"And where will you go?"

"I was thinking of going up to the Vega," I said.

"The Vega? What for?"

"To see it," I said. "It's the only part of the country I haven't seen."

"In my humble opinion it is the only part of the country not worth seeing. It is very poor and arid. The people are rude. The food is bad. There is nothing to see. It is cooler up there, yes: that is all that it's good for."

"Surely there must be something. There must be a town, or something. Villages."

"Of course there is a town. One town—Encampo. Totally without charm. And several villages, quite squalid. It is not a place for someone like you to visit."

"What do you mean, someone like me?"

"I mean there is no Hotel Excelsior up there."

"I do not want that. I want to get away from all that for a day or two. I don't mind roughing it."

Ali laughed. He stood and picked up my empty espresso cup. "Another?" he asked.

"No," I said. "I know you think I'm some sort of effete American, but I'm not. Or I wasn't always. I've slept out-of-doors, beneath the stars, on the ground, before. And quite enjoyed it."

"Like a cowboy," Ali suggested.

"Not quite," I said. "Just tell me, how does one get up there? Should I take the railway?"

"Yes," said Ali. "There is a bus that leaves every morning and evening from behind the train station, but it takes forever and is always blowing a tire or falling into a precipice. And it is full of people coming and going from market. You will not like that. Take the funicular and the cog railway. They were made in Switzerland for people like you."

"Ali, if you weren't so nice to me, I would think you disdained me," I said.

"Oh, rest assured that I do," said Ali. "In my business, the two are by no means mutually exclusive."

"How cruel you are," I said.

"Yes," he said. "Very cruel."

He got up and prepared me another espresso, to belie his cruelness. "This one is my treat," he said, and handed me the small, steaming cup.

"Thank you," I said.

He rolled another cigarette, sat smoking it.

"There is really nothing to see?" I asked, after a moment. "What about in the villages? No churches, or castles, or handicrafts?"

"Handicrafts! Don't sound so much like an American! You are deluded. It is not at all picturesque in that way. Go. You will see."

As it was getting late when I concluded my talk with Ali, I decided to wait and begin my trip in the morning, so I would arrive in Encampo in daylight.

The cog railway took me from the fifth terrace up through the foothills to the base of the cliff, where the track terminated and everyone rushed across a little platform and pressed themselves into the waiting funicular. I had second thoughts, for it appeared to be nothing more than a large wooden box suspended on tired cable. My trepidation was well-founded: the box quivered all the way up, while the cable groaned. Everyone was silent and tight-faced, as if any additional movement or sound would bring the whole thing crashing down. Under other circumstances the view would have been amazing: La Plata had always seemed to me a city of heights, but rising up from it against the sheer wall of cliff flattened it out, and I could see for once how truly tiny it was: the harbor, the peninsula, the town built up in concentric rings of red, and all of it surrounded by the mountains, as if God had taken a teaspoon and scooped a little of them away.

Yet the tininess of it all disconcerted me. I had been feeling settled and safe; I had thought that I had done not a bad job of establishing a new life in just a few weeks—I had made friends, and I had found myself a beautiful place to live—but as I watched La Plata shrink below me, I realized my new life could disappear just as easily, how everything is finally only a matter of perspective.

Suddenly the box came to a shuddering halt and the doors opened onto terra firma. There was a little shrine, with a plaster Mary in a garden of plastic flowers, right outside the terminus, and as the passengers exited, they crossed themselves and kissed the statue on the top of her slightly bowed head. It all seemed very unhygienic to me, and absurd: to court illness only moments after escaping death.

Ali was right: Encampo was a dreary place. The old city had been flattened and rebuilt as a result of the late Mr. Quay's Upland Initiative, and all the buildings were designed in the most hideous architectural styles of the 1960s: a lot of poured concrete and white glazed bricks. It had none of the antique charm of La Plata, and its citizens seemed disheartened by their environment: there was a sort of scouring glumness about them: they were civil, but unfriendly. The market square, which stood directly outside the rail terminus, was a sun-scorched, asphalt-covered lot; dirty water of various disturbing hues pooled around sewers, and all the food was rotting or rotten. The vendors behind the stalls looked defeated, as if they knew how unappetizing their wares were.

For a moment I considered finding a place to have some lunch and then taking the next train back down to La Plata, as there really did seem to be nothing to see or do and the place was having a depressing effect upon my spirits. And despite what Ali had said, it seemed much hotter up here than in La Plata: there was no sea breeze. But some sort of stubborn pride compelled me to stay. I had spoiled myself with La Plata; a day or two in the real world would do me no harm. It would be good for me.

There were apparently no decent hotels in Encampo, but Ali had given me the name of a woman—Esmeralda St. Pitt—who rented guest rooms in her house. I decided to find this place first and leave my bag there, before I explored any more of the town.

Since Encampo was laid out in a grid and its streets were lettered or numbered, it was not very difficult to find the St. Pitt residence. It was one of many identical semidetached houses on a quiet street.

Its door was answered by a regal-looking woman of African descent. She wore a caftan of gold-and-green fabric, and had her hair bound up in a scarf made of the same material. "Yes," she said.

"Are you Mrs. St. Pitt?" I asked.

"Yes," she said.

"My name is Alex Fox. I come to you at the suggestion of Ali Haffid. He suggested you may have a room I can rent for a night or two."

She looked me over and then said, "Are you a friend of Ali's?"

"Yes," I said. "I suppose so. I am living in the apartment above his shop."

"I don't rent to just anyone," she said. "This is a family home." She touched the wall of the vestibule, which was covered in garish paper: a background of metallic gold on which grew a trellis of flocked velvet grapes. "A family home," she repeated, with special emphasis on the family.

"I'm not sure what you mean by that," I said.

She ignored this comment. "Is that your only bag?" she asked, nodding at the small leather valise I held.

"Yes," I said.

"I have two rooms," she said. "I will show you both and you will have to decide which of them you want. I cannot decide for you. They're upstairs." She stood away from the door, which she opened all the way, and I stepped into the vestibule. "Upstairs," she said again, and I followed her up a narrow flight of stairs, onto a little landing. Directly in front of us a door opened into an immaculate bathroom; on either side of us doors opened to reveal two small identical bedrooms. "Which do you want?" she asked.

I walked into the room on my right. It looked as clean as the bathroom and was furnished modestly but tastefully. "This would be fine," I said. "How much per night?"

She named a price, which included breakfast. It seemed a bit high, but I was in no mood to argue or barter. I put my bag down on the bed. She stood in the hall, watching me for a moment, as if I might do something deviant which would disqualify me from staying in her family home. After a moment she reached into a pocket of her caftan and removed a key, which she held out to me. "Breakfast is at 7:30," she said. "I'll fetch you some fresh towels."

I spent a rather stultifying afternoon wandering around Encampo. There really was nothing to see. Finally I gave it up and found a café with tables set out beneath a green plastic awning and I sat there drinking beer. I returned to Mrs. St. Pitt's about five, and took a nap, from which I awoke in a groggy stupor two hours later. I lay on the small narrow bed and wondered where I was. I was beginning to have this odd feeling, after waking up, as if I had awakened in the wrong place, as if there was some other place in the world where I was supposed to be, almost as if my life back in the United States was continuing in some disembodied way without me. By moving away from so much that was familiar, I sometimes felt unnervingly insubstantial.

After a moment I heard the door across the hall open and someone enter the bathroom. Mrs. St. Pitt must have found another guest. I heard the noisy rumble of the bath being filled, and then the swish of displaced water as a body—a large body, by the sound of it—was lowered into the tub.

I wanted to take a bath and clean myself up before I ventured out for dinner, and I waited for the other guest to finish in the bathroom. I heard the water being sucked out of the tub, and then the bathroom door opened and I heard footsteps in the hall. I waited a moment or two and then donned the robe that Mrs. St. Pitt had thoughtfully hung on a hook behind the door and ventured into the hall. At the same time that I opened my door, the door to the other bedroom opened, revealing Mr. Dent. I was shocked to see him, and for a moment I stood there stupidly, thinking that he could not be real. But he was.

"Alex," he said. "What in God's name are you doing here?"

"I just came up for a day or two to see things," I said. "What are you doing here? I thought you were in Ibiza. Is Ricky with you?"

"No," he said. "She's still over there. I've come back early. I'm up here to—Well, it's a long story. Why don't you take your bath? I hope I've left it clean enough for you. Do you have plans for dinner? Perhaps you could join me."

"That would be fine," I said.

"It's good to see you," he said. "I've got a lot to tell you."

Mr. Dent took me to El Grotto, an Italian restaurant in the base-ment of a building right off the market square. The ceilings were low and vaulted, and we were seated in a dark little alcove, lit only by the candle on the table. "So what are you doing here?" I asked him, after we had ordered our meal and received our bottle of Chianti.

"Oh," he said. "I hardly know. I'm in a bit of a muddle."

"What's gone wrong?" I said.

He was fiddling with the cork, gouging little crescents into its soft flesh with his thumbnail. "Do you remember what you told me the other night?" he asked.

"Not really," I said.

"You said there was no reason why I shouldn't be happy. That I should pursue my life more honestly."

"Did I?"

"Yes," he said. "You did."

"Well, it sounds like good advice. But don't put too much stake on anything I tell you. I've made a mess of my life."

"Have you?" he asked. He set the cork aside and looked over at me.

"Yes," I said. "In fact I have."

"But you seem so poised and in control."

"Appearances can be deceiving," I said.

"I suppose," he said.

"What's this all about?" I asked. "Is there trouble between you and Ricky? Is that why you left her in Ibiza?"

"We've decided to separate for a while."

"Why?" I asked. There was something about the dark grotto that encouraged confidences.

"Why? Why does any couple separate? Because they're not happy together. We've been struggling for a while, and I suppose we're both tired of struggling. I think maybe we'll be happier apart, that if I leave her, Ricky can start again with someone. I'm no good for her. I can't go on failing her."

"But she loves you," I said. "She's told me so."

"It's because I'm all she has. But I really think it would be better if I left her."

"Does she agree?"

"She's as miserable as I. We agreed it was worth trying. So I returned before her to pack up my things and leave."

"Where are you going?"

"I'm not sure. Do you know Barcelona?"

"I do not," I said.

We were interrupted by the arrival of our antipasto: a large glass plate on which was haphazardly arranged an unappetizing selection of pickled vegetables and tinned meats.

"So I'm going to Barcelona. Or trying to go to Barcelona."

"But what are you doing up here in Encampo? Isn't it out of your way?"

"Yes," he said. "You're right. You see, something's come up that's making it difficult for me to get away."

I didn't ask what. I knew he would tell me. I forked a few olives and peppers onto my plate.

After a moment he said, "Apparently the police want to speak with me."

"About what?" I asked.

"About these murders. The bodies in the harbor."

"Why would they want to speak to you?"

"I'm not sure. There was a summons waiting at home for me, asking me to report directly to Police Headquarters for investigative questioning. I suppose I'm some sort of suspect or something, because they know I was wandering about alone all that night. If only Ricky hadn't panicked and reported me missing."

"Did you talk to them?"

"No."

"Why not?"

"I'm scared."

"What are you scared of?" I asked.

"I don't know, really. That they'll arrest me, I suppose. And convict me, and I'll spend the rest of my life rotting in jail. Andorra's something of a police state, you know. Everything is fine until you get on the wrong side of them. I've had some trouble with the police before."

"Trouble about what?"

"Oh, ridiculous charges of indecent behavior. 'Public lewdness.' Totally unfounded, of course. It happened at the locker room out at the beach club. They send their husky young recruits in there to entrap pathetic men like me. If you so much as ask them the time of day, they arrest you. And once they've established you're a degenerate, I'm sure it isn't hard for them to imagine you're a murderer."

"So instead of going to the police you've come up here?"

"Yes," he said. "I just want to get out of this damned country and go to Spain. If I took the train from La Plata I'd have to show my passport and I'm sure they'd detain me. I thought I'd come up here and try to get out over the mountains."

"How?" I asked.

"Hiking, I suppose. It can't be too difficult."

"But if you leave in that way it's tantamount to admitting your guilt. You'll never be able to come back. I don't advise it. And it's impractical, if not impossible. You cannot hike over these mountains."

"You'd be surprised what you can do when you need to do it."

"That's nonsense. Do you have any sort of mountain-climbing experience? Any equipment?"

"No."

"Then you would perish."

"I'd be willing to take that risk. Perishing doesn't seem such a bad idea. I probably should have done it long ago."

"Listen to me," I said. "Don't be a fool. Go back and talk to them. Get yourself a good lawyer and talk to them. I'm sure nothing will come of it. Perhaps you aren't a suspect at all. Perhaps they only want to question you. They may think you saw something, wandering around that night."

"Perhaps," he said. "But it's a risk."

"It's much less of a risk than fleeing across the Pyrenees to Spain. And what about Ricky? Shouldn't you talk to her about all this?"

"She's rather disgusted with me at the moment. She wanted me gone before she came back."

"Nevertheless, I'm sure she'd want to help you with this. Can you get in touch with her?"

"No," he said. "There's no telephone at the place we were staying."

"Well, when is she due back?"

"In about a week's time."

"You can't wait that long. We'll go back down to La Plata tomorrow, and you'll send word to Ricky to come home immediately. We'll get you a lawyer—I know one: Edward Darlingham. He's the man the Quays use, so he must be the best. And then we'll go talk to the police. You've got to face this squarely and resolve it. You can't run away."

"I suppose you're right," he said. "It's very good of you to help me like this. It's extraordinary, really, my meeting you up here like this. A miracle. I can't say what it means to me."

"Say nothing, then." I poured more wine in his glass. "Relax," I told him. "Drink up. Everything will be fine."

It was chilly by the time we returned to Mrs. St. Pitt's. There was no sign of our hostess. Mr. Dent and I said good night on the little landing at the top of the stairs, after agreeing that he would use the bathroom first. While I waited for him to finish I opened the window and stuck my head out into the cool night air. There was really nothing to see: just the dark windows of the neighboring house, and below a little alley filled with trash cans. Up above a glittering swathe of stars.

And then a tap on my door: "It's all yours. Good night."

Something woke me in the middle of the night. I lay in bed, and heard stealthy noises from across the hall. Ricky was up: he opened the door to the hall and I heard him outside my door, and then I saw a note emerge beneath it. At the sound of his footsteps on the stairs, I immediately got out of bed and turned on the light. The envelope had the following message scrawled on its exterior:

Alex—Could you see that my wife receives this note? I'd be forever grateful. Don't be too disappointed in me. I've enjoyed our
brief friendship, and think the world of you.

All my best,
Richard Dent

I tossed the note on the bed, threw on my clothes, and ran down
the stairs, only to encounter the formidable figure of Mrs. St. Pitt
standing in the vestibule. "I don't know what's going on, but I
won't allow it. I told you both this was a family house. A family
house! And I won't have you coming and going all night. I won't
have it."

"Listen," I said. "I'm sorry. This is most unusual, but I really
must go after Mr. Dent. I think he's in some danger."

"Danger!" she exclaimed. "What kind of men are you?"

"We are both decent men," I said. "But he is in danger and I
must go after him."

"I won't let you back in! You can come back in the morning for
your things. At a decent time, mind you. I've had it with the lot of
you. I'm going to bolt the door when you leave, and if you try to
get back in tonight I'll call the police."

"Fine," I said. "I'll return in the morning."

The street was empty. I ran down it just in time to see Ricky
Dent hastening across the deserted market square. What a sad sight:
a man running away in the middle of the night. I ran faster and
called out to him.

He turned around as he heard me approach. "Please don't follow
me," he said.

"I have no intention of following you," I said. "I'm here to stop you and bring you back with me. Where are you going?"

"You know where I am going." He began walking up a street that seemed to lead out of town.

I fell into step beside him. "I thought you saw the foolishness of that plan," I said.

"I do. Yet it is the only plan that makes any sense for me."

I grabbed his arm in an attempt to stop him, but he shook me off and continued walking. I fell into step beside him. "It makes no sense. You said you would come back and talk to the police and get in touch with Ricky. That is the plan that makes sense. You've got to go back and face up to all of this," I said. "At least stop walking for a moment."

He was carrying a little leather valise. He put it down on the street beside his feet and reached inside his coat and extracted a handkerchief, with which he mopped his brow. It was a chilly, damp night, but he was sweating.

"Come back with me," I said. "You can't just run away."

"Yes," he said, "I can." He folded the handkerchief and stuck it back into his pocket. "I'm walking out to Lanjarón. That's the village where I taught music. It's in the foothills. I'll find somebody there who can help me over the mountains. I have some friends there, some good decent people who know the mountains and will help me. Did you see the note I left you?"

"Yes," I said. "I left it back in the room."

"But you'll give it to Ricky?"

"Of course," I said.

"I've got to go," he said. He picked up the valise, but stood there.

"You can get out of this," I said. "With a good lawyer, if there's no physical evidence — they'll have no case against you."

"Do you think I killed those men?"

"I don't know," I said. "Perhaps you did."

He looked at me. "Do you really think I might have killed someone?"

"No," I said. "Of course not, and that's why you should come back with me. Innocent men don't flee."

He smiled a strange, sad smile. "You have no idea how justice works," he said. "Or how it doesn't work. Please give the note to Ricky and forget you ever met me. But I won't forget I met you, and I won't forget how you've tried to help me. Thank you for that." He held out his hand.

I shook it. I couldn't think of what else to do. I shook his hand and watched him walk to the end of the street. I watched him disappear around the corner.

ᴪ

THE ONLY BUILDING THAT WAS OPEN AT THAT EARLY HOUR WAS
the church, which seemed, coincidentally, to be the only building
in Encampo which had been spared the brutalizing and modern-
izing influences of the Upland Initiative. There were no pews, only
dozens of beautifully carved wooden chairs arranged in rows, and
I sat on one of these and looked up at the altar. Two brightly
painted urns held bouquets of plastic flowers. Exhausted Jesus was
nailed to a cross: a large wooden cross with a large wooden Jesus,
rough-hewn and primitively painted. His face was simple, but eloquent in its simplicity, eloquent with a sort of calm anguish, an
anguish that had been sustained for so long it was no longer really
felt but simply borne.

I said to myself, sitting there, *I am not a religious person,* as if
to assure or remind myself. I said it out loud. I don't know why I
feel the need to steel myself against religion, as if against disease.
As if it were something I could get without wanting. I don't know
why, because I admire people who have faith. I envy them, in fact.
I am intrigued by intelligent people who are religious. I knew a
woman in San Francisco, an accomplished journalist, a woman
who had traveled all over the world and who could write intelli-
gently about almost anyone or anything, a scholar, a feminist. And

this woman was a devout Roman Catholic. Once I asked her how she reconciled her intellect and her faith, and she told me that she did not.

They are separate bowls, she said. One for the soul and one for the mind.

So you believe with your soul and think with your mind? I asked her. Was it like patting your head and rubbing your stomach?

No, she said. It's not that simple. Don't be so literal. They are not really separate. They are not separate at all. I believe with my heart and my soul and my mind. Otherwise it would mean nothing.

But how can you do that? How can you believe in something that your intellect does not corroborate?

But that is what belief is, she told me. We believe in what we cannot know or understand. We do not believe in what we know.

I suppose this woman had a capacity, or perhaps simply a need, for belief that I don't have. But it seemed unfair to me; it seemed inherently wrong that belief was a talent bestowed upon some and denied others. Like singing.

And I sat for a long while in the little church, looking at the wooden Jesus. I hoped that it would speak to me. I wish I lived in a world in which statues spoke. I remember when I was young, I traveled with my parents to Rome. I think it was Rome. There was a sort of statue: a huge flat face with a hole for a mouth. You stuck your hand into this hole, and legend proclaimed that if you had told a lie your hand would be bitten off. And I remember inching my hand into the dark mouth with real trepidation, for I knew I had told lies, and in some obscure yet real way I believed my little boy's hand with its delicate sparrow-like bones might be severed. I was old enough to know better, but I was still young enough to believe. It is a shame that we so quickly lose that ability to believe in things; it limits the opportunities we have to transform ourselves, to save ourselves, for it puts the awful burden of transforming and saving ourselves on ourselves. Once you stop believing, you cannot pray, or make sacrifices or pilgrimages, or light candles. You are stuck with yourself, in a world without miracles.

After a while I left the church and sat in a café near the market, drinking watery coffee until a "decent hour," when I returned to Mrs. St. Pitt's for my things. I rang the bell and waited on the little stoop. I was beginning to think the hour was not decent enough for Mrs. St. Pitt when she opened the door, glowered fiercely at me, thrust my bag into my arms, and quickly closed the door.

I stood there on the stoop, stunned by her aggressive sanctimony. I could not bear being treated with such disdain, so I set the bag down and reached out and touched the bell. After a moment the lace curtain at the window beside the door moved, revealing part of Mrs. St. Pitt's large face. I motioned for her to come to the door. She shook her head and disappeared, yet I would not let myself be disposed of so easily. I rang the bell again, and kept it pressed until the door opened.

"Mr. Fox," said Mrs. St. Pitt, "if you don't stop this at once I'll call the police. And believe me, my threats are not idle ones."

"I don't doubt you. I merely wanted to explain to you the events of last night, as you seem to have misconstrued them and your treatment of me is unacceptable. If you are the decent woman you claim to be, surely you will hear me out."

"I am always willing to listen to anyone," she said, "provided they talk with courtesy and reason. Why don't you come into the parlor?"

"That is very kind of you," I said, and followed her through the vestibule. She sat on a sofa that was occupied by many pillows with inspirational slogans needlepointed on them. MANY HANDS MAKE RIGHT WORK, I read, and another proclaimed in words spiraling out from the center, in a rainbow of colors, CHARITY BEGINS AT HOME BUT EXTENDS EVER OUTWARD. I sat on an overstuffed but lumpishly uncomfortable chair opposite her.

"I am sorry if I appeared unreasonable last night," said Mrs. St. Pitt. "But I simply cannot tolerate the sort of activity you and your friend engaged in. If my neighbors complain about my guests, which I assure you they do not hesitate to do, I am in serious danger of losing my license, and consequently my livelihood. I had no choice but to turn you out. In fact, I would never have allowed you to stay had I known that you were lovers given to quarreling."

"I understand," I said. "But I am afraid you have grossly and unjustly misinterpreted my relationship to Mr. Dent and the events of the night."

"I should think the events speak for themselves," said Mrs. St. Pitt.

"To fools perhaps they do. But wise men — and women — know better."

"You are calling me a fool?"

"I am," I said.

"And I think you are a dishonorable and rude man."

"I'm sure I am. But I was not last night. Last night I was nothing more than a gentleman and a friend. Allow me to explain."

"I am, as they say, all ears."

"You see, yesterday I was sent up here from La Plata to find Mr. Dent and convey to him a message, a message I am sure that you, a woman sensitive to family feeling, will understand the importance of: his daughter, his three-year-old daughter was very sick, and it was urgent that Mr. Dent return at once to see her. There was the fear that she might die. As I found him too late in the day to return to La Plata, we planned to take the first train in the morning. But apparently Mr. Dent woke in the night from a terrible dream in which he saw his daughter reaching out for him. Not thinking clearly, he imagined that he would return immediately to La Plata on foot, and ran from your house. The commotion of his exit woke me, as it woke you, and I, knowing the hysterical state he was in, feared he might do some harm to himself and raced after him."

"The poor man!" exclaimed Mrs. St. Pitt. "I trust you found him."

"I did," I said, "and I managed to calm him, and we waited at the station for the first train."

"And I turned you out of my house! Shame on me. If you had explained the situation, I would have behaved differently."

"I had no time. I thought it best to chase after my friend."

"And to think I locked my door behind you! How uncharitable of me. But there is a detail of your story that confuses me. You say your friend is called Dent?"

"Yes," I said.

"Mr. Dent?" she said. "That is most odd." She stood, crossed the room, and stepped into the vestibule, where she consulted a guest book that was lying open on a little table. "He did not sign in as Mr. Dent. Here he has signed in as—yes, as Mr. Greensleaves. Joanne—no: Johannes Greensleaves. An odd name. And you say he is really called Mr. Dent?"

I got up to look at the little book, as if there might be some mistake. But the evidence was irrefutable: there, just below my own illegible signature was carefully printed *Johannes Greensleaves.*

"It is a little odd," I said. "But then people often use a false name when registering at hotels."

"Do they? I don't see why they should. And this is not a hotel. This is a family house. I do not welcome guests under false pretenses. I feel not a little deceived by your friend."

"I have no explanation to make. I can only assure you that I know Mr. Dent is a decent man, and I am sure he had no intention of deceiving you. Traveling gives us an opportunity to reinvent ourselves, to take on new personas."

"If we are decent people, we should have no need to reinvent ourselves. One persona should suffice," said Mrs. Pitt.

"You are right," I said. "I can make no excuses for my friend."

"Well," she said, "I'm sorry about the whole episode. Will you stay for breakfast? It was included in the price of your stay."

"Thank you, but no. I am anxious to get back to La Plata."

"I'm sure you are," she said. "The poor dear girl. I shall pray for her. I hope you will come to stay with me another time, a happier time. It is your right and my obligation. Anytime you wish to stay with me, Mr. Fox, you will be my guest. And I mean that in the truest, most Christian sense of the word."

"You are very kind," I said. I shook her hand. "God bless you."

When I arrived, later that morning, at No. 16 San Julián de Loria, I stepped out onto the terrace and looked down at the town and the harbor as if to make sure they were still there and had not been rolled up and taken away overnight. It was all there, intact, as lovely as ever, yet try as I might to saturate my mind with the images before me, I could not forget the sight of Mr. Dent hastening up the deserted street into what was left of the darkness, like a refugee, a castoff from Paradise.

CHAPTER THIRTEEN

A FEW AFTERNOONS LATER, I FELL ASLEEP ON THE BEACH AT Crowespoint and was awakened by a sprinkling of cold water on my hot back. I turned over and looked up, but the figure above me was silhouetted by the sun and I couldn't discern its identity. Then it crouched down beside me and revealed itself to be Mrs. Dent. "Fancy meeting you here," she said.

I was a bit groggy from my sleep. "Hello," I said. "You're back."

"Just," she said. "I arrived this morning. And felt that awful incapacitating depression of returning home. I decided a swim might rejuvenate me. You're looking well. How bronzed you are! Spending a bit of time on the beach, are we?"

"Yes," I said. "I've been here the last few afternoons."

"Well, it seems to agree with you. Do you mind if I plonk myself down beside you? Or would you rather be alone?"

"Not at all," I said. "It's good to see you again. I missed you."

"Did you?" she said. She stood up, extracted a folded towel from her straw beach bag, shook it, and smoothed it out over the sand. Then she sat down. She rummaged in her bag for a tube of tanning cream, which she rubbed onto her legs and arms. She held the tube out to me. "Will you do my back?" she asked, turning a little on the towel to show me the V of bare skin her bathing suit revealed.

"Of course," I said. I took the cream from her and rubbed some into her flesh. "You don't look as if you need this," I said. "You're darker than ever."

"Yes," she said. "I rather baked myself in Ibiza. But it's good for the skin. The cream, not the sun. Thanks," she said, as I finished. "Do you want some? Your shoulders are looking a bit lobstery."

"Yes," I said. She rubbed the cream into my shoulders in a sort of brisk, unerotic way, as if she were a nurse. Then she returned the tube to her bag and lay on her stomach on the towel. She was wearing a navy-blue one-piece bathing suit with a gold-link belt around the waist, a straw hat with a blue-and-white bandanna tied around its brim, and big round white-framed sunglasses. She looked quite fit and beautiful.

"How's the water?" she asked, sifting some sand through her fingers.

"Nice," I said. "Warm."

"It was almost too warm in Ibiza," she said. "I didn't like it. It wasn't really refreshing."

"How was your trip?" I asked.

She opened her fingers and allowed the sand to pour through them, and then brushed her hands together. "Oh, it was fine," she said. "It's nice to get away. I should do it more. How have you been?"

"Fine," I said. "How's Ricky?" I asked. I was curious to hear what she'd say.

"Actually, I'm not quite sure," she said. "We've decided to split up for a while. Nothing permanent or treacherous, just a while apart. So he's off somewhere — Barcelona, I think. He left Ibiza before me."

"Actually, I saw him," I said.

"You did? When?"

"A few days ago," I said.

"Where? Did he come to see you?"

"No. I bumped into him. Up in Encampo."

"Encampo?" She turned over and sat up. "What was he doing up there?"

"Leaving the country," I said.

"I know," she said. "But through Encampo?"

"Yes," I said. "He was trying to get out of the country over the mountains. He was afraid to take the train because the police were looking for him."

"Why were the police looking for him?"

"Remember the body they found in the harbor that night he was missing? The night before you left for Ibiza? They thought he might know something about that and wanted to question him."

"Even so, I don't understand. Why was he fleeing over the mountains?"

"He was scared. Panicked. He said he had had trouble with the police and thought it best to avoid them."

"But it's impossible! You can't hike over those mountains."

"That's what I told him. I tried to stop him. I told him to come back down here and speak with the police. He wouldn't listen to me."

"But surely you didn't let him go! It would be criminal to allow someone to hike over the mountains!"

"What was I to do?"

"Talk sense to him. Restrain him if necessary."

"I told you, I tried to talk to him. I got out of my bed in the middle of the night and chased after him. You must believe that I did everything I could short of physically restraining him. He's a bigger and stronger man than I. And in any case, he was dead set on what he was doing. There was no changing his mind. And as impossible as it seems, I think he's safe. Seeing him walk off like that, I just have a feeling he's safe."

"How did he seem to you? When you saw him?"

"Fine. A bit preoccupied, but in retrospect, under the circumstances, that makes sense."

"What circumstances?"

"I mean your separating, his going away."

"Did he tell you about that?"

"Yes. In fact he did."

"Then why did you ask me about him like that? Why did you pretend not to know?"

"I wanted to give you the liberty of telling me some other story if you wanted to. I wasn't sure you'd want me to know."

"Of course I would. It's nothing I'm ashamed of. Do you think I should be?"

"No," I said. "He left you a note. He gave me a note to give you."

"Did he? You haven't got it with you, have you?"

"No. It's back at my house. It must still be in my bag."

"Can we go look? Now? Surely you've had enough sun."

"All right," I said. "Just let me rinse off. Don't you want a swim?"

"No," she said.

I left her downstairs and went up to look for the note. It was stuffed into a little zippered pocket on the inside of the valise. I brought it downstairs.

Ricky was standing out on the terrace. I handed her the note. She looked at it for a moment and then used her fingernail to slit the envelope. I sat in the living room while she read, but watched her through the open French doors. It was only a page long, but she must have reread it over and over, for she stood there holding it for quite some time. Then she sat down at the table.

I stood in the doorway. "What does he say?" I asked.

She looked up at me. Her face looked drained, stricken.

"What?" she said.

"His note," I said. "What does he say?"

The note was on the table and she reached out and touched it, lightly, with her fingertips. "It's over," she said.

"What?"

"Everything," she said. "Our marriage. He says he doesn't want to come back, and he doesn't want to see me again. He wants to start a new life, and thinks I should do the same. That it would be better that way."

"Is that not what you want?"

She didn't seem to hear me.

"Would you like a drink?" I asked.

"What?"

"Could I get you a drink? You look like you could use a drink."

She shook her head no, and then, after a moment, she said, "I'm sorry. Do you think you could leave me alone for a moment? Just a moment."

"Of course," I said. "I'll be upstairs. I'm going to take a shower."

When I came downstairs after my shower she was gone.

It was a warm, quiet night. The breeze had stopped and everything was still. Often, at odd moments, the town—at least the third terrace—seemed like this: deserted, in abeyance, hushed. And then I heard the sound of spraying water and looked down into the interior courtyard to see Ali hosing the flagstones, chasing the debris into the gutter, which ran down the middle of the alley and into the street. When he was finished he carefully coiled the hose around the spigot and then disappeared around the front of the building. I heard him pull down the metal awning of his shop, and then all was quiet again.

I decided to take a walk. I went into the Hotel Excelsior; I thought I might find Mrs. Reinhardt and read to her awhile, which would be a calming and pleasant finish to the day, but she was nowhere about. I left her a note at the reception desk, asking her to contact me so that we could arrange a meeting, and then pushed through the revolving doors out onto the plaza. People were seated around the rim of the fountain, eating ice-cream cones, holding the cones up and sucking delicately at the melting ice cream through the pointed tips, like nursing calves. I went into the confectioners and ordered a cone (cassis) and walked with it up onto the harbor promenade. The tables outside the cantina were full of beautiful laughing men and women. I didn't like the cantina at night: it was hard to book a table, and everyone who sat there looked on display, the women in their lovely summer dresses, the men with their hair oiled back on their heads, their tanned bare feet resting proprietorially on top of their Gucci loafers. One wanted to applaud them for presenting such a successful vision of life: you could almost believe they had lived their whole lives, had been reared and groomed from birth, for this one particular night: that this was the pinnacle, this golden summery evening they had all reached simultaneously.

Yet it made me a little sad to see them there, laughing and drinking champagne, for you knew it was all downhill from here.

I recognized Nancy Quay Flyte Bottom at a crowded, boisterous table. She looked very beautiful: she had her hair up and rather large diamonds in her ears. Her dress was cut low enough to reveal the untanned tops of her breasts. As I watched, she shook a cigarette out of a little silver case and held it in her mouth while a gentleman lit it. She turned away and exhaled a great cloud of bluish smoke, and saw me. She waved, and I lifted my ice-cream cone in an imbecilic salute. She motioned for me to join her table, but I wasn't at all in the mood, so I smiled and shook my head no. She waved again, somewhat dismissively, and returned her attention to her many friends.

I walked to the end of the wall, which curved out into the harbor, separating it from the open sea, and stood there, looking out at the world. There must have been a dance or some sort of fête at the beach club: it was all lit up, and I could hear faint strains of dance music blowing across the water. A couple who had been standing in the shadows next to me began to dance, moving dreamily to the faraway music. The man smiled at me over his partner's bare shoulder — *aren't I the lucky one* — moved his hand lower down her back, and closed his eyes. I turned around and left them there.

I recrossed the plaza and walked up the alley that ran behind the opera house. The stage door was open and music leaked from it. *Nabucco*: Act III, the Chorus of the Israelites. I peered inside, and I could see the stage through the wings, crowded with Jews stranded on the banks of the Euphrates, longing to return to their homeland. *Va, pensiero, sull'ali dorate.* It was, I realized, the controversial production I had read about the day I arrived. The Jews were costumed in pale-green body stockings that totally obscured their faces and bodies, and stood with their arms raised above them, undulating rhythmically like sea grass swaying in a current. A stagehand saw me standing there and came and closed the door, not wanting me to have something for free. I remembered singing for Mr. Dent in the summerhouse, how the notes had risen up from somewhere deep inside me, pure and on pitch.

I wasn't eager to get home, so I tried to get lost; I walked haphazardly up streets and alleys and staircases, but it was really too small a place to get lost in: I kept turning a corner and realizing I knew where I was.

My wanderings had by this time brought me to the fourth terrace, and I found myself in the immediate neighborhood of the casa Dent. It was late to pay a visit, but I decided to walk by the house and see if any lamps were still lit. A soft glow emanated from inside the living room, but no one answered my knock. And then I heard a faint breeze of music from the back yard. I walked around the house and stepped over the gate, so as not to cause the bell to ring and Dino to bark. My quiet approach allowed me to observe Mrs. Dent for a moment before announcing myself: she sat inside the summerhouse, and Dino sat beside her, his massive head on her lap. On the table were the usual candle, gramophone, and bottle of iced wine. Mrs. Dent sat quietly, apparently lost in thought, stroking Dino's head. She looked sad, and a little defeated. I watched her until the music stopped, and when she stood up to turn the record over, I knocked on the frame of the screen door. She looked up and saw me. "Ah," she said, "it's you."

"May I come in?" I asked.

"Of course you may."

I opened the screen door and stepped up into the little room. Mrs. Dent concentrated on the gramophone, and when she had the record playing again she sat down. "Sit down," she said. "Would you like a glass of wine? I trust you've found yourself dinner."

"I did, thank you," I said. "I've just been out for a walk."

"It's a lovely night," she said. "Too lovely to go indoors."

"Yes," I said.

"Do you want some wine?" she asked.

"Please," I said.

"I've only one glass," she said. "I wasn't expecting you. Let me get you one. I'll be right back."

"No," I said. "You stay here. I'll get the glass."

"They're in the cabinet above the sink," she said.

I returned with a glass and poured myself some wine. We sat for a moment in silence, listening to the music. When I looked up at

Ricky, I saw that tears were rolling down her cheeks. She bent forward and laid her head on top of the dog's, holding his head in her hands. Dino whimpered a little but sat still. His face reminded me of the wooden Jesus of Encampo. I stood up and put my hand on Ricky's back, which was shaking softly. The record finished, but it continued to spin on the turntable, and the gramophone hissed. After a moment, I reached over and turned it off, and then the only sounds were Dino whimpering and the trees murmuring outside the screened walls. I sat back down.

"What's the matter?" I asked. "What's wrong?"

"Everything," she said.

"Tell me," I said.

"Ricky went away because I told him something in Ibiza. Something I don't think I should have told him. You see, it's for me that he went away, not for himself."

"But I thought you agreed to spend some time apart—"

"No," she said. "That was his idea. And now he's gone for good. I've lost him."

"You can't be sure of that," I said.

She said nothing.

"What did you tell him, in Ibiza?"

She looked at me. "I told him I loved you," she said.

That night we slept in her bed, in the small bedroom at the end of the hall with the chiming clock. We made love carefully and tenderly, as if we were both fragile, as if the act of inflicting our bodies on one another was as full of danger as it was bliss.

CHAPTER FOURTEEN

*F*OR A WHILE AFTER THAT I KEPT COMPANY WITH MRS. DENT, spending most days (and nights) with her. The days we spent at the beach and the nights we spent—in every sense of the word—in the maharajah's bed. They were indolent, sunstruck days, and in retrospect I am sure they will come to seem my happiest days in Andorra. Yet there were shadows, and I could not walk through them without sensing a warning—or an instruction: These days are finite. They will come, like a season, to an end.

One night I woke to find myself alone in bed. I went downstairs and saw Ricky sitting out on the terrace, on a chair drawn up to the mosaicked table beside the fountain. She was wearing Uncle Roderick's dressing gown and smoking a cigarette. I had never seen her smoke before.

The moon was huge and round, hung up over the sea like something cheap and ornamental. I walked out onto the terrace and sat beside her. "Where did you get that?" I asked, nodding at her cigarette.

"I bought some the other day at the tobacconists. You can pick the tobacco and they hand-roll them for you. By the dozen. I was just passing by and got the urge. I haven't smoked in years. It's quite good. Turkish." She held it out to me, but I shook my head.

"Couldn't you sleep?" I asked.

"No," she said.

"Why not?"

"I don't know," she said. She took a last drag on the cigarette and then stubbed it out in a celadon ceramic teacup. It irked me that Ricky was treating it as an ashtray.

"You shouldn't be using that," I said. "It's a teacup."

"I couldn't find an ashtray," she said. "I'll clean it."

"It's just that I've got to be careful of all these things," I said. I reached across the table and flicked some tobacco off the sheared-mouton collar of the dressing gown. "You're messing everything up," I said.

"Oh, I am not. If you're going to be cranky, go back to bed. Leave me alone."

I leaned closer and slipped my hand into the front of the gown and palmed one of her breasts. It felt warm and alive in my hand, and I could feel her heartbeat in it. She placed her hand on top of mine, linked her fingers through mine, but just for a moment, before withdrawing both our hands. She placed my hand on the table, which felt cold and damp compared to her breast.

After a moment she said, "What are you doing here?"

"I woke up and you weren't there. I came to look for you."

"No," she said. "I mean, what are you doing here? In Andorra. What brought you here?"

I remembered our first conversation at the cantina: *Say the wind brought you, or fate . . .*

"Fear," I said.

"Fear of what?"

"Fear of staying where I was," I said.

She waited a moment. She pulled a piece of tobacco from her lips and flicked it to the ground. She somehow managed to do this in a delicate way that was not unattractive. "How did your wife die?" She said this in a careful, neutral voice, as if she were only being polite, as if this were the next question of a long and tedious survey.

"My wife?"

"Yes." Her voice rose with impatience. "I believe you had a wife. You told me she died. But perhaps it's all lies. Perhaps you've never had a wife. Who knows? Perhaps you have several. Who knows anything about you? You lay beside me at night and it frightens me how little I know you."

"I lie beside you," I said. "I don't lay beside you."

She glared at me.

"My wife died," I said. "As I told you. I had one wife and she died."

We were both quiet for a moment, and then: "How did your wife die?"

"She killed herself," I said. "My wife was mad. She also killed our daughter."

"Oh my God," Ricky said. She took another hand-rolled cigarette from the pocket of Uncle Roderick's gown and lit it with a little onyx lighter shaped like a chesspiece. A knight: she stroked its mane and the yellow flame whooshed from its nostrils. I had seen this bibelot on the bookshelf and never realized it was a lighter. Suddenly I had the feeling that all the objects in Uncle Roderick's house were masquerading. Ricky held the cigarette between two fingers in front of her mouth for a moment, her remaining fingers delicately splayed, like a woman in an advertisement.

"Please don't smoke," I said. "I don't like it that you smoke."

She put out her cigarette.

"Thank you," I said.

"You're welcome," she said. She took a few more cigarettes out of the dressing-gown pocket and pitched them, one by one, over the parapet. I actually remember saying that to myself, hearing it in my head: *She pitched her cigarettes over the parapet.* As if language were a comfort.

"It was partly my fault, what happened," I said. "I betrayed my wife."

"You fell in love with someone else?"

"Yes," I said.

"That is not the worst thing in the world," said Ricky.

"In the way that it happened to us, it was," I said.

"But it hardly makes you responsible for what she did," said Ricky.

I did not answer.

"Tell me about her," said Ricky.

"What do you want to know?"

"I don't know. I just want you to talk about her. You keep so much inside. Was she pretty?"

"Yes," I said.

"Describe her."

I tried to picture Helen, but what came to my mind was the body in the morgue, the yellow sheet, the gash like a single gill on its bloated neck.

"Why do you want me to talk about my wife?" I asked.

"Because I think it would be good for you. For us. It's a little unnatural not to. Was she pretty?"

"Why do you want to know if she was pretty?"

"I don't. I'm just trying to get you to say something. How did you meet her?"

"In graduate school. Architecture school."

"You're an architect?"

"Yes."

"I thought you owned a bookstore."

"I did. I gave up architecture after a while. We inherited a lot of money when Helen's father died, and we stopped working. Well, we bought the bookstore. That is where I met Laurel."

"Who is Laurel?"

"The woman I fell in love with. Or thought I was in love with."

"Were you?"

"No."

"But you thought you were?"

"Yes."

"And your wife thought you were?"

"Yes. She thought it before me, I think. It's how I came to realize it: seeing her see it."

"And she was jealous?"

"No, not really jealous. It was sadder and weirder than that. Something happened to her after Anna was born. It was something chemical, I think, but she wouldn't do anything about it. She was nursing Anna, you see, so she wouldn't take anything. It was a matter of pride for her."

"Yes," said Ricky.

"I tried to help her," I said. "But she got paranoid and violent. She killed our cat. I told her I was going to commit her, but before I could, she killed herself. And Anna."

"What an awful story," said Ricky. "But it sounds as if you did all that you could do. What else could you have done?"

"I could have not fallen in love with Laurel."

"It doesn't sound as if it was really about that. And besides, people make mistakes. People should be forgiven for the mistakes they make, not punished for them. You say yourself she was mad. You did not make her mad. People don't have that power over others."

"But I feel responsible."

"Well, I can't tell you what to feel. You must feel what you must feel."

"I want to get over it, though," I said. I looked at her. "It's why I came to Andorra. How do I get over it?"

"I don't mean to be cruel, but I think you're a little stupid. You get over it in the way you get over it," she said. "Or perhaps you don't get over it. I don't know. Perhaps you aren't meant to get over it. What does it mean to get over something like that? To forget it?"

"No," I said. "To live with it. To be able to live with it."

She reached out and touched me. "But that's exactly what you are doing," she said. "Isn't it?"

"Yes," I said. "I suppose."

She leaned back into her chair. She straightened the two tails of the dressing gown's sash across her lap, and then studied the result. "Did you know I had a son?"

"No," I said.

She looked up at me. "I thought Ricky might have told you. We did. He died in an accident at an amusement park. He wasn't buckled into a ride properly. Not at all, in fact. His name was Jon Antony. Jon: J-O-N. No H. He was seven years old. He was so beautiful. We came to Andorra to try to forget about it—get over it, as you say—but, well, you don't. You can't. And why should you? What's the point of it all if you forget?"

"I don't know," I said.

We sat there for a while in silence. The moon had risen higher in the sky and shrunk a little.

"I'm sorry about your son," I said.

She shrugged. "I didn't tell you so you'd be sorry for me," she said.

"I know," I said.

"I suppose that's when our marriage really ended," she said. "But we tried to go on together. To comfort one another. It's an awful thing to lose a child. Well, you know. How old was your daughter?"

"Eighteen months," I said.

"A baby," she said. "How could anyone kill a baby?"

"I don't know," I said.

Mrs. Dent shivered.

"It's chilly," I said. "Let's go back to bed."

She reached across the table for my hand. "Yes," she said. "Let's."

$\mathcal{T}$HE BIBLIOTECA STOOD ON A QUIET STREET ONE BLOCK OFF the plaza. Upon closer inspection, it appeared somewhat like a diminutive municipal building, the somber back of which it faced: the same colonnaded façade, the same domed roof, and, of course, the same faded red granite. Inside a set of double doors and down a short dark corridor, I entered a large, glass-domed circular central hall. About twelve desks, all piled high with books, were arranged like the hours of the clock around the room's circumference, and at its center stood a circular ottoman, on whose brocade-upholstered lap sat more piles of books. Glass doors opened off this room to the back and the two sides of the buildings, and through these doors I could see dimly lighted rooms of shelved books. Stairs in one corner led up to a balcony directly beneath the dome, and glass-fronted cabinets filled with books lined this circular gallery, inscribing an octagon into the sphere.

Of the dozen desks in the central hall, only three were occupied: two o'clock, five o'clock, and ten o'clock. These people—two men and a woman—were all involved in the activity of lifting a book from one pile, and perusing its interior. I noticed the woman carefully sniffing each book, inserting her formidable nose deep into its gutter, examining its dust jacket, spine, and boards, making some notation in pencil on the endpaper, and moving it to another pile. When it became apparent that no one was going to acknowledge me, I decided to approach one of the people at the desks. The woman was attractive in a wild, unkempt way: fat, with a lot of red hennaed hair pinned up on top of her head, most of which had already escaped. Her eyes were ringed with kohl. She scared me. One man was young—my age—and the other was older—maybe sixty. I decided to approach my peer, who sat at ten o'clock. He was a small, neat, handsome man, with close-cropped dark hair and small wire-rimmed glasses. He wore a seersucker suit that was a little short in both the arms and legs, and a bow tie. He was looking through a large book of what appeared to me to be Felice Beato photographs. I stood before his desk and said, "Excuse me."

"Yes," he said. "Can I help you?"

"I hope you can," I said. "I've only recently arrived in Andorra, and as I'm interested in books, a friend mentioned the Biblioteca, and I thought I would stop by and see how it operates. She also informed me about the civil service. I would like to inquire about participating in that as well."

"Why don't you sit down?" said the man. He stood and withdrew the chair from the neighboring desk and pushed it beside his own. "Please, be seated."

I sat down.

"So you are interested in books?" he asked, as he reseated himself.

"Yes," I said. "I had a bookstore in San Francisco. An antiquarian bookstore."

"Did you have a specialty?"

"Yes," I said. "We specialized in incunabula and books about photography and architecture. And first editions of American and British literature."

"An interesting mix," he said. "Well, the Biblioteca is not a bookstore. It is, more precisely, a book exchange."

"An exchange?" I asked.

"Yes," he said. "What happens is that people bring in their unwanted books, which are appraised by me or by one of my colleagues. They are assigned a value, which is expressed in a certain number of points: one hundred, let us say. Those books are then catalogued and shelved according to their subject and value, and the one hundred points are credited to the account of that client, who may at that time or at any time thereafter exchange those one hundred points for a book or books of equal value. The purpose of the institution is to recognize the worth of good books, but also to recognize their purpose, which is to be shared and read often by many people."

"And people are willing to give up their valuable books?"

"We deal in books of all values. But as for valuable books, yes, people are willing to give them up, because they get equally valuable books in return."

"And what if the client disagrees with the appraisal?"

"That rarely happens. The Biblioteca prides itself on the expertise of its appraisers. But when it does, the book is considered by two other appraisers, one of whom is always the director. Those appraisals are averaged with the original appraisal. If this final value is not acceptable to the client, the matter is closed, the book returned."

"And are you employed here, or are you doing your civil service?"

"I am an employee. Most people doing civil service here work in administration, book restoration, or building maintenance."

"If I were interested in becoming an appraiser, what would I do?"

"Well, you would have to take an examination. It is difficult. There are three parts: an exhaustive test of general literary knowledge; an essay you must write on an area of book publishing or collecting in which you have special expertise; and then a trial appraisal of three books culled randomly from our shelves. If you do not pass the examination but score well, you may become an assistant to an appraiser."

"Well, I would like to be an appraiser. I should like to take the test," I said.

"It must be scheduled. If you see Miss Ying, in the director's office down the hall, she will make an appointment for you."

I stood up. "You've been most helpful," I said. "Thank you very much."

He shook my hand and said, "My name is Søren Pan. Let me give you my card in case you have further questions." He opened a drawer of his desk and extracted a calling card with the following engraved on it:

Søren Pan
4 Square Alain Fournier, La Plata 1, Andorra

The first person I saw upon entering the director's office was none other than Miss Quay. She was kneeling on the worn linoleum floor, transferring books from a low shelf onto a wheeled cart. She saw me as I entered the room and stood up. "Mr. Fox!" she exclaimed. "What are you doing here?"

I explained to her my presence in her midst, and asked her what brought her to the Biblioteca.

"I have just begun to do my civil service here," she said. "I was working in the Mortal Children's Hospital, but that—well, unless one is a saint, one can't do that sort of work forever. I felt in need of a reprieve and thought working with books would make a nice change."

"Are you an appraiser?" I asked.

"Heavens, no," she said. "I have not that sort of expertise. I've done a little book maintenance and restoration, which I enjoy, but mostly I have been shelving books and maintaining records. And making tea for Herr Franck, our director. You say you are here to see Miss Ying?"

"Yes. I was told to see her about making an appointment for the exam."

"I'm afraid she's out to lunch. But I expect she will be back before too long. I was about to bring these books up to the rotunda. Have you seen the rotunda?"

"I have only glimpsed it from below."

She invited me to accompany her and began to push the little cart, which was laden now with books, out into the corridor. I was interested to see her away from Quayside and the interfering presence of her family. She seemed more animated and confident, and the low-watted gloom of the Biblioteca lent her eyes and skin a radiance; her beauty, which sometimes seemed defeated, shone.

I followed her through the circular hall and into a little alcove. She opened the gate to an ancient bird-cage elevator that was hardly bigger than a dumbwaiter, and pushed the cart into it, which left little room. "Perhaps you should take the stairs," she suggested. "I'll meet you on the gallery."

I recrossed the hall and trotted up the stairs. Miss Quay ascended in the elevator. I opened the gate and helped her extract the cart.

"These are all new acquisitions," she said. "The most valuable books are kept up here in these cases, under lock and key. They are not available for exchange."

The books I had glimpsed through the glass doors certainly merited this treatment. Most of them appeared to be extremely rare books, leather-bound, deckle-edged. I remember the first time I realized that books were not unique, like paintings: I was at a birthday party and the birthday boy received as a gift a book I knew was mine; it was on my bookshelf at home, and I insisted it be returned to me. And I remember the birthday boy's mother condescendingly explaining to me that there were many copies of this book extant in the world. I had never heard anything so idiotic or foolish, but her willingness to lie to procure gifts for her illiterate son amazed me into submission. And when I returned home I found the book back on my shelf, where I knew it belonged, and I thought some sort of miracle had occurred: that the woman's lying had caused the book to leave their wicked house and make its way back to mine, like a lost animal that is mistreated or unloved by subsequent owners and makes an incredible journey across frontiers to return to its original home.

So you can see I was stupid about books from an early age.

Miss Quay and I made our way around the gallery. I pushed the little cart, and she unlocked the cabinets and interred the precious books.

"We have missed you at Quayside," Miss Quay said. "You once promised to be a frequent visitor. What have you been doing with yourself?"

"Not very much of anything," I said. "That's why I'm here at the Biblioteca, seeking to make some better use of my time. I hope I pass the test so I may join you here. I would enjoy that."

"You wouldn't see much of me. The appraisers tend to treat everyone else here with marked disdain."

"I would not."

"We can only wait and see."

Between every large bookcase there was a small dormer window, which extended out from just below the base of the dome. I looked out the window closest to us and saw a walled garden directly behind the Biblioteca. A fountain stood at its center, and flowering trees lined four narrow alleys, which extended from its corners to the fountain. "What is that?" I asked, pointing out the window.

Miss Quay stepped closer and looked. "Oh," she said. "That is the War Memorial Garden. The Crowes built it to honor the memory of their son who was killed in the Spanish Civil War. He and five others. I often like to sit in it. It's one of the most tranquil places in La Plata."

"It looks lovely," I said.

"Would you like to see it?" she asked. "I mean, to visit it?"

"Now?" I asked.

"Of course."

"What about your work?"

"Oh, I am allowed to take a break. That is one of the perquisites of working voluntarily. Let's sit outside for a moment."

She left the cart on the balcony and I followed her down the stairs, through one of the dimly lit rooms of books on the ground floor. She pushed aside heavy velvet drapes that covered French doors, and opened them out into the quiet garden.

We walked up one of the narrow shrouded alleys to the fountain. In the middle of a six-sided basin a bronze angel stood knee-deep in water. She held an urn in her arms, from which water slowly poured into the basin, where it overflowed and cascaded into a little gully that ran around the fountain's base. As we came nearer, I noticed that a name was inscribed on each side of the basin's rim, a name that could be read through the thin sheet of water that continually flowed over it. The name we stood before was GUY CARLETON CROWE: 1910–1936. "This is the Crowe boy," she said. "My mother loved him when she was young. I once found a packet of letters he had written her from Spain. They were very beautiful. You can't imagine. Or perhaps you can. I could not. They made me so sad, for I couldn't imagine my father ever writing such letters to my mother."

"Did they not love one another?" I asked.

"Perhaps they did, early on. But I never felt it," said Miss Quay. "Theirs was a relationship of tolerance and respect. They had separate bedrooms. And then those passionate, tragic letters up in the attic. It is difficult to reconcile."

"I believe our parents' lives are always difficult to reconcile," I said.

"I suppose all lives are, finally," said Miss Quay. She looked at me and smiled. "I always seem to have such gloomy conversations with you! You must think me a very morose woman."

"I think you a very thoughtful woman."

She continued to regard me. The canopy of trees caused the sun to mottle her face in a way that was not unbecoming: she wore a sort of transparent, shimmering veil. "And beautiful," I added, because it was true.

She blushed and looked back at the fountain. "Come," she said. "I'll show you my favorite name." I followed her halfway around the fountain and she pointed at a name, DEMETRIUS SKY. Miss Quay reached her long, beautiful fingers into the water and touched the letters. The water divided around her fingers, rearing back up into sparkling furrows. "Isn't that a beautiful name? Of course, all the names of men who die young in war become beautiful. Whenever I see a memorial plaque I always stop and read the names. All of them. Quietly, out loud. In France they are everywhere, in every town." She withdrew her hand from the basin, flicked some water from her fingers, and looked around the little garden. "I used to come here often, but I stopped—"

"Why?" I asked.

"I think of my brother here. I suppose because he, too, died young."

"I didn't know you had a brother," I said. I looked at her, but she wasn't looking at me: she was watching the water spill from the angel's urn, emptying but never empty.

"Yes," she said. "He was named Augustus Edward, but we called him Gus."

"When did he die?" I asked.

For a moment she said nothing, and the only sound was the water falling into the basin. But then she spoke: "About ten years ago." She turned to look at me. Her face was composed. "He killed himself. Of course we don't talk about it, don't mention it. That's probably why I hang on to him so. Sometimes I go and sit in his room. Nothing's been touched. The clothes in his closet still smell of him. Faintly, but surely. There's even a book on his nightstand: *Bel-Ami*. With a bookmark! He died without finishing it."

She turned back toward the angel in the fountain and put her hand in the basin. She observed it there, through the magnifying lens of the water, as if it were a curiosity, or an amulet, something that could save her in a flood if a flood were to come. I reached my hand into the water and floated it near to hers. The water was cold. Our two hands, in the water. Slowly, almost imperceptibly, I swam my hand toward her hand and touched it. I was about to hold it when she withdrew her hand, hurriedly, with a little splash. It dripped some dark moist beads onto her dress. She stood for a moment, composing herself, and then she said, "I'm sorry."

"Sorry? Why are you sorry?"

She seemed unsure what to say. She held her wet hand in her dry one, as if it were injured. "I don't know," she said. "I'm confused."

"Confused about what?"

"About you, I suppose. I don't really understand you . . . and it . . . it confuses me."

"What don't you understand?" I asked.

She looked at her hand. "Nancy told me she sees you often with a woman. The Australian woman with the large dog."

"Mrs. Dent," I said. "She is my friend."

"Your friend?"

"Yes. Mrs. Dent is my friend. I think I mentioned her when I came to lunch at Quayside. I have been spending some time with her lately, because she's unhappy. Her husband has left her, and she is sad and lonely."

"And so you comfort her?"

"To the extent that I can, I do."

Miss Quay was silent a moment. The dark stains on her dress had already dried in the bright sun. She said, "I suppose I wonder what form your comfort takes."

"You mean, you wonder if I sleep with her?"

She looked at me. She actually seemed to shake a little, although it might have been leafy shadows wavering across her face. "I do, although I suppose it is none of my business. It's only that, well, as I said, I'm confused. The attention you've paid me — has confused me. And I don't know what to do. Nancy says — "

"What does Nancy say?"

"No. I don't care what Nancy says! Nancy has always — "

"What has Nancy told you about me?"

"I told you that I don't care what Nancy says. I care what you say." She looked at me.

"What I say about what?"

A look of anger or impatience crossed her face. "Oh, it is hopeless," she said. "I am hopeless at this. I do it all wrong! I feel that I am pushing you, that you really have nothing to say to me, and I am making a fool of myself."

"You are doing none of those things," I said.

"Well, I feel that I am, so it little matters."

"It matters a great deal," I said. I took a step toward her. "It matters—" I began, but then I stopped. I reached out and touched her hand, and then grasped her long fingers and held them. "Sometimes," I said, "people think they can explain themselves to one another by talking. That they can explain their feelings for one another as they happen, almost as they occur. A sort of simultaneous translation of thoughts and feelings; they think that there should be no mystery, that everything between them should be articulated, understood. It is, I think, what you are trying to do now. You are trying to understand me and how you feel about me and how I feel about you by talking to me and asking me to explain myself. I understand your motivation, because I, too, am confused. But your questions scare me, as do my answers; they seem so reductive and final. I am still discovering what I feel for you. All I know is that it is a great deal, and I feel it with warmth. And passion. But it is dark, a forest, a dark forest, and I do not want to start chopping down all the trees so that I can see them and explain them. I love this darkness we are in."

"You love the darkness?"

"Well, perhaps love is the wrong word. I respect it. I honor it."

She removed her hand from my clutch and went and sat on one

of the benches that lined the alleys. I stood for a moment at the fountain, and then I went and sat on the bench opposite her. We faced one another across the path of gravel and shadow.

"All my life I have felt a little in the dark," said Miss Quay. "And not only a little, sometimes. And I neither love nor honor nor respect it: I hate it. So it would seem we are incompatible."

"I think you misunderstood me. I didn't mean that we should stay in that darkness forever. I only meant that as a stage in our relationship, it should be honored and not rushed."

"And for how long must we loiter in your honorable yet extremely dark forest?"

"I'm sorry. I was trying to explain something to you, and perhaps I made a stupid analogy. I have trouble explaining myself, especially to people I care about."

"But I never asked you to explain yourself! I wouldn't presume to ask you that. None of us can explain ourselves."

"If we can't explain ourselves, then how do we become understood, and absolved?"

"Absolved? Are you seeking absolution?"

"Yes. The absolution that comes from being completely understood and accepted by another human being."

"Hadn't you better look to God for that?"

"But I don't believe in God. So I must seek absolution in my temporal relationships."

"So your friends must also be your saviors? Isn't that a rather large burden to place on them?"

"I don't think helping those we love through the world is a burden," I said.

"But surely there is a difference between helping a friend and saving a friend."

"Maybe not," I said. "How do we know? We can never know what constitutes salvation for another person."

"Perhaps you are right," she said.

"Do you believe in salvation?"

"I'm not sure what you mean by salvation."

"Salvation is a sort of reassurance that one has not lived idly or in vain. That one's life has some sort of spiritual purpose and design."

"Then, no, to answer your question, I don't believe in salvation. I do think we live idly and in vain. In fact, I think it is a little presumptuous to think otherwise."

"But then why are you alive?"

"What do you mean?"

"What is the point of being alive if you think that?"

"There is no point to it. It merely happens. My life is quite pointless, and that is fine with me. It makes it easier to bear." She stood up. "I should return to my books." But she did not go. She stood there.

"I believe it is possible to find salvation through love," I said. "Have you ever been in love?" I asked.

"Yes," she said. "Once."

"And did you feel saved?"

"Saved? Saved from what?"

"From the fear that you were an awful person."

She shook her head. "I never feared I was an awful person. No, love did not save me from that."

After a moment she said, "Do you have that fear?"

"Yes," I said.

"You are afraid you are an awful person?"

"Yes," I said.

"Why?"

"I have done awful things," I said.

"What things?" she asked.

I said nothing.

"Have you hurt people?"

"Yes," I said.

"Who?"

"My wife. And my child. And other people, too. I am not a good person."

She sat down on my bench and touched my hand with hers. "Perhaps you were not a good person. But what does that mean? Who is always good? No one. Saints, perhaps. But you are a good person now. Right now. You have been kind to me."

She moved on the bench; she shifted and reached with her hand and touched my face, and I realized there were tears on my cheeks. She brushed them away and then placed her hand on the back of my head. She gently pushed it down onto her shoulder. I felt the material of her dress against my cheek. And smelt the clean lineny smell of her.

It will be all right, she was saying. It will be all right.

CHAPTER SIXTEEN

A DAY OR TWO LATER A LETTER ARRIVED FROM QUAYSIDE. IT read as follows:

My dear Alex—

I hope this finds you in good health and spirits. We have missed your company of late but realize you must be as busy as we during this high summer season. There was a time when civilized people retired from society during the summer, but those times seem sadly—like so much!—to be a thing of the past.

I write you with a proposition that I hope will meet with your liking and approval. My dear (dear!) friend Isolta Fallowfield has invited us (as she does every summer) to voyage with her a week or two on her yacht, the *Splendora*. We go neither far nor fast— simply where the wind and our whims carry us. We plan to head east this year and may get as far as Turkey, a country which I, for one, would dearly love to see—but tssk! my desires are of no matter, except where they pertain to you:

Isolta has asked me to invite any sympathetic friends, as her boat is large and her party small—merely her son, Vere, a delightful young man. Of course I immediately thought of you. Isolta will arrive in La Plata in three days time from Formentera; she plans to spend a day or two here at Quayside, and then we would all depart for glorious (one hopes) points east in about a week's time—most probably on Tuesday, the 15th. We should return to Andorra sometime around the end of this month, or the very beginning of the next.

Isolta is a lovely, generous, charming woman. She is a friend of my youth, and a dearer woman simply doesn't exist. (A fact!) I know you will adore her, and she you. So say you will come — it will really be the most marvelous time, and made all that much better if you join us.

I look forward to your reply. Jean has just entered the room and asks me to send you her affection. Consider it seconded, and sent.

À bientôt—

I put the letter down and thought about how odd life was: how getting things you wanted was mostly a matter of proximity and circumstance. The nearer one got to the pinnacle, the faster one's ascent. Yet it scared me a little, to get what I wanted, for I knew I wanted some of the wrong things. It was a sort of damp shivery fright, but I knew how to cure it: I stepped out onto the terrace and sat in the hot afternoon sun. I closed my eyes, lifted my face to the sky, and let the sun bake the fear out of me.

It was the closing night of the ballet, and there was to be a gala benefit at the opera house that night. Ricky had gotten it into her head that we should go. In fact, she had bought the tickets without conferring with me and simply announced that we would be in attendance. This was a tactic of hers, I now realized: as we fumbled our way through our private relationship, she arranged for us to appear together in public as often as possible, as if such exposure, like sunlight for the jaundiced babe, was therapeutic. As if being a happy couple was simply a matter of publicly appearing as one.

As I entered her house that evening, Ricky called to me from the bedroom. I walked down the Hall of the Chiming Clock and stood in the doorway. She was seated at a little dressing table, clipping rings to her ears. She looked at me in the mirror and said, "You look fabulous, darling. I don't know why men don't wear tuxedos all the time. They're so sexy."

I walked over and put my hands on her beautiful bare shoulders. She was wearing a black crêpe de chine dress with a tightly fitted bodice and a great flounce of a skirt. I kissed one of her tan shoulders, which smelt of fragrance and powder, and then bit it just a little.

"Don't!" she said. "You'll leave a mark."

"You look beautiful," I said.

"Well, I'm trying," she said. "What do you think of these earrings?"

"They're fine."

"Do they look all right with the shoes?" She stuck one of her feet out from beneath the canopy of the dress: it was a black silk pump with a gold band around the top and bottom of the French heel.

"They're perfect," I said.

"Which?" she asked. "The shoes or the earrings?"

"Both," I said. "Everything. You."

"I'm not going to wear any other jewelry," she said. "Do you think I should?"

"No," I said. "You look very elegant and beautiful as is. Don't gild the lily." I kissed her shoulder again.

"Don't bite!" she warned.

I sat down on the bed behind her and watched her put on lipstick and face powder. I have always liked watching a woman do her makeup. It is as if you are backstage before a performance. Helen wore very little makeup. None, in fact. She was, and knew she was, beautiful without it. So was Ricky, but there was something about her willingness to try and transform herself with makeup—I suppose it is a lack of confidence, a dependence on artifice—that I found human and endearing. After all, it is a little vain to assume you don't need makeup. Everyone does.

"I received an interesting letter today," I said.

"From Ricky?" She stopped powdering and looked at me in the mirror. Despite the powder—or perhaps because of it?—she suddenly looked pale.

"Ricky? No. From Mrs. Sophonsobia Quay."

"Oh," she said. She returned the puff to the compact and snapped it shut. "What did the old bear want?"

"It was an invitation. To go on a cruise with them, on a friend's yacht."

"I didn't know you were that friendly with the Quays."

"Neither did I," I said. "That's why I said that the letter was odd."

"You didn't say odd. You said interesting."

"Well, it's both: odd and interesting."

"You're not going to go, are you?" She reopened the compact, studied her face in the mirror, and touched the puff to her forehead and cheeks. Her eyes met mine in the mirror.

"I don't know. I think I might like to. How many other chances will I have to cruise the Mediterranean on a private yacht? Don't you think it's too fabulous an invitation to decline?"

"What about me?"

"I'll only be gone for a week or two," I said.

"That's not what I meant. I meant, why can't I come as well? As your guest?"

"Well, Mrs. Quay didn't mention anything about you."

"Don't be dim. Of course she didn't. But you could mention something to her, couldn't you, about me? That you'd like to bring a friend along?"

"I think that would be rude," I said. "Mrs. Quay has asked me individually. I must respect the nature of the invitation."

"This is exactly what I meant!" She turned away from the mirror and looked directly at me. "This is why I told you to stay away from the Quays. I knew they would cause problems."

"I don't really see how this is a problem. If they invited me to dinner, would you be so upset?"

"No," she said.

"Well, I think this invitation is just as casual."

"Oh, don't be an idiot. Of course it's not. They're asking you to travel with them for a fortnight. I suppose Jean will be on board?"

"I'm not sure."

"Of course she will be. And I'm sure Mrs. Quay will do everything she can to throw the two of you together."

"I've already told you what an absurd idea that is. I wish you would just forget it."

"I'm sure you do."

"Ricky," I said, "I don't want to argue about this. If you don't want me to go with the Quays, I won't. It's as simple as that. But I don't want you to stop me because you are jealous of Miss Quay. That would be nonsense, and it would hurt you, I think, eventually. Hurt both of us. If you have a good reason for me not to go, tell me and I won't go."

"When are they leaving?"

"Not for a week. But I'm supposed to respond immediately."

"Immediately? How like them. Surely they can wait a day or two."

"I think it would be polite to respond tomorrow. If I decline, I'm sure they will seek someone else out."

"All right, then. I can't think about this now. Let's go to this bloody gala. I'll tell you in the morning."

"No," I said. "Tell me now. Please. Otherwise, I won't enjoy the gala. I'll be preoccupied."

"I don't see why this should be my decision. In fact, it isn't, and I refuse to be manipulated into thinking that it is. It's your decision. Go on the cruise if you want. It's fine with me."

"Is it? Really?"

"Yes," she said. "In fact, I could use some time alone." She turned back to the mirror. "I was going to put my hair up," she said, "but fuck it."

Outside the opera house an expensively dressed crowd of people nervously and gaily chattered, all doing their best to look at one another while not appearing to do so. The women's hair looked like pastry, twisted and rolled and marcelled into sugary nimbuses about their beautiful heads. In fact, there was something confectionery about all the women—their Necco-colored gowns, their bare dusted flesh, all of them smelling of vetiver or hibiscus—something that made one's mouth water.

We made our way silently through the crowd, like strangers at a party, and entered the theater. We moved through the gas-lit lobby, up the grand staircase, and into the salon, a room with a glass-brick floor which allowed the light that flowed in through the glass ceiling to penetrate to the lobby level below. Circular ottomans upholstered in red velvet and festooned in gold braid stood about the room, and huge glass-and-iron doors were opened onto a balcony that overlooked the plaza.

I snagged two flutes of champagne from a passing tray and we carried them out to the balcony. The same crowd we had pressed ourselves through remained below us, and we leaned on the balustrade and gazed down at them. It was that odd time of day when the light goes all soft and benevolent. I looked out over the plaza: the light of the setting sun fell so thickly it seemed to be holding up the façade of the Hotel Excelsior, as if when it subtracted itself into nothing at the horizon the entire hotel would come crashing down in the dusk. A few people hastened across the plaza, on their hurried way somewhere for something, and a few tables outside the cantina were occupied by eagerly amorous couples who couldn't wait for the night to begin. And something about the combination of the light and the champagne and the height and the perfumed evening air intoxicated me; I was suddenly overcome with a sort of fizzy and debilitatingly stupid happiness. An external happiness, a site-specific happiness, a happiness that occurs sometimes when I feel I am in the right place at the right time, when the world around me seems so perfect, so artfully poised and displayed, like a boutique window, that I give in to it: I believe in its perfection, and I feel safe and excused, as if the loveliness of the visible world somehow precludes anything bad that could happen to me. I suppose everyone feels this; I suppose this is why we travel, why we pack trunks and book berths, why we visit cathedrals and castles, why we stand on veldts and lidos, clutching our cameras and Baedekers, assuring ourselves that the certified magnificence of what we see somehow includes or involves us, and we soak it all in, only to have it leak from us as we sleep between freshly laundered hotel sheets.

Ricky was not happy. I could tell this by looking at her: she stood beside me, sipping her champagne, gazing down at the crowd below us with a stricken expression. I recognized it as her look of defeat, an expression that every now and then obscured her lovely open face, like ugly scaffolding on a beautiful building.

I was about to say something to cheer her when the gong began gonging and we entered the gilded theater and found our worn velvet seats. The interior of the opera house was the kind of space that made you feel the world was over. Or that the best part of the world, the pinnacle, the time when such theaters could be built, had existed without you and would never come again.

An acquaintance of mine has tried to convince me that this architectural nostalgia of mine is deluded and pathetic, not to mention anti-democratic. He explained to me that the beautiful things of the Old World I was always gushing on about were built as a result of unpardonable tyranny and suffering: the gold and rosewood and mother-of-pearl all plundered from brutally colonized countries; the natives forced down into the mines or up into the trees.

I suppose he was right, but the fact that he lived in a meticulously restored Willis Polk villa on Vallejo Street and owned a sixteenth-century castle in Umbria somehow made his argument less convincing, for it is easy to denounce the beauty of the Old World when you possess it.

This final program of the ballet season was a surreal and giddy collage of highlights from the repertoire. It seemed to me a program devoted to showing how inane the world of classical ballet is, how far removed from our own. And after a while I gave up on the marzipan spectacle on the stage and turned to watch Ricky watch the dance. Her face looked lovely and rapt, bathed in the soft stage light, and as Albrecht lifted Giselle—or who knows? it may have been Romeo lifting his Juliet—above his head and carried her across the stage, her impossibly long legs flexed and extended before and behind them like the prow and stern of a ship, her head raised, her face transfigured by simulated moonlight, Ricky began to cry, silently and stilly, the tears rolling down her face, rounding her cheekbones and cascading down the long flank of her cheeks, irrigating smooth channels through the powder. I reached out and found her hand in her lap; she let me hold it, but continued to watch the dancers, and as I looked back at them, at the marvelous boat of them sailing across the stage, I realized that ballet works not by counterfeiting the world we know but by showing us a world better than, different from, revelatory of, our own.

· · ·

Ricky said she didn't feel well, so we skipped the post-performance supper and walked up the quiet stairs and streets to the fourth terrace. We loitered on her front porch beneath the arched trellis of papaya bougainvillaea. She reached out and touched, but did not turn, the doorknob. She touched it reverently, as if it were an amulet, something that could save her in a flood if a flood were to come. "I think I'll leave you here," she said.

"Ah," I said. We had been silent on the walk home. For much of the evening, in fact.

"Yes," she said. She looked up at me, shyly, like a girl on a date, and I did feel as if I loved her not a little. "I think the champagne gave me a headache. It often does. I'd like to be alone tonight."

"Are you tired?" I asked.

"Yes," she said. She yawned as if to illustrate this fact.

"Will you be all right? Is there anything I can get you?"

"Oh no. I'll go right to bed."

"All right," I said. "I'll say good night, then." I leaned forward to kiss her and she offered me her cheek.

"Good night," she said. She opened the door and disappeared inside. A light went on in the hall and then another in the living room. A breeze shook the bougainvillaea, and some tired blossoms flurried to the ground. I stood on the stoop for a moment and then walked down the brick walk, but I realized I had no desire to go home alone, so I turned and followed the path around the side of the house. I opened the gate in the wall, stilling the bell with my hand so it wouldn't ring, and there was something odd about my hand on the bell, as if I had put it on someone's mouth to silence a scream. I crossed the lawn and entered the summerhouse. I'll just sit here awhile, I thought. Just sit here and think. In the cool, companionable darkness.

The Victrola crouched on the table. In the shadows it looked like some odd little beast.

Down yonder green valleys . . . where twilight is fading . . .

After a moment a lamp snapped on outside the back door, casting a little pool of light across the lawn, but luckily it did not extend as far as the summerhouse. The door opened and Dino bounded down the steps and began rooting about in the bushes. I heard the relieved hiss of his urination. Ricky stood just outside the door, looking up at the night sky. I knew it was wrong to watch her in this voyeuristic way; I had not meant to spy. Really, I had not. Dino emerged from the bushes and wandered close to the summerhouse. He must have smelt me, for he came and stood on the steps. He whined and scratched at the screen door.

"Dino," Ricky called. "Come. Come, Dino darling. Mummy's tired."

But Dino continued to whine and scratch.

I made a quiet growling noise at him, hoping it would scare him away, but it only served to pique his interest.

"Dino!" Ricky stepped down into the pool of light in her fabulous dress, like an actress entering from the wings. She walked through it and stopped at its edge, about fifteen feet from the summerhouse. "Who's there?" she asked.

I stood up and moved toward the screen, so she could see me. "It's me," I said. "I'm sorry if I scared you. I didn't mean to."

"What are you doing in there?" she asked.

"I didn't want to go home. I thought I'd just sit in here awhile. I wanted to stay near to you."

We stood there for a moment, with the screen between us.

"I'm sorry if I was rude before," she said. "Not asking you in. It's only that I'm confused and wanted to be alone."

"I understand," I said.

"Do you?"

"Yes," I said.

"Good," she said. "Actually, I'm a bit angry at you, I think."

"About the cruise?"

"Yes," she said. "Although now I don't know. Perhaps I'm the one being selfish. I mean, you're right: why shouldn't you go on the cruise if you want? It's wrong of me to want that. And I understand that it's unlikely they'd ask me to accompany you. I just wish . . ."

"What?"

"I wish—and I know this is selfish of me, but it is what I wish— I wish you didn't want to go. I wish you wanted to stay here, with me."

"It's only for a week or two," I said.

She sighed. "It's not really the amount of time."

"You mustn't be jealous," I said.

"That's an absurd thing to say to someone," she said. She shrugged. "I am jealous."

"But there's absolutely no reason for you to be jealous."

"Perhaps," she said. "But jealousy isn't the most logical emotion."

"I can't not go on this cruise to make you happy."

"I know," she said. "Go on the cruise. I'm sick of it. Let's not discuss it anymore." She reached out and grasped Dino's collar. "I'm going to bed. I wish you'd leave. I really don't want you lurking about my garden."

"Why are you so angry?" I asked.

"I'm not angry! I'm tired. And perhaps a little angry. Maybe I'm not even angry with you. Maybe I'm angry at myself. I don't know. I don't want to explain it. I just want to go to bed. Come, Dino."

She turned around and, pulling Dino, began to walk toward the house. She paused about halfway, beside the stone birdbath, and turned toward me. "You've failed me," she said. "And I'm a little sad. It's only natural. You see, I think when one falls in love with someone, one waits to be failed. You sort of hold your breath and wait, because you know it's coming. It's like you're driving in a car and you know there's going to be an accident, only you don't know when."

"That's an odd description of love," I said.

"Yes," she said, "I suppose it is."

"I don't see how I've failed you."

She laughed: it was an odd, sad laugh.

"Why are you laughing?" I asked.

"Because I'm relieved," she said. "It's over between us. You know that, don't you?"

"No," I said. "I don't see why it should be."

"Of course you don't. You're not a very sensitive person. Sensitive to yourself, perhaps, inordinately so, I think, but not to others. Is this how you treated your wife?"

I said nothing.

"I'm sorry," she said. "Now I'm being mean. It's over: let's just leave it at that."

She turned around again and began walking toward the house, but when I called out her name she stopped.

"What?" she said in an exhausted way.

"Come sit with me in the summerhouse. One last time. Just for a while?"

"Why?" she asked. She continued to face away from me.

"Because it is a beautiful night. Because I don't want to leave you in this way. Because it is the place where I was most happy with you."

She considered. I watched her bare back, lovely and tense in the moonlight. It relaxed. She let go of Dino's collar. "All right," she said. "But let me get a shawl. It's chilly."

I offered her my jacket, but she refused. I watched her go into the house. A light went on in the bedroom and after a moment it went off. And then the outside light snapped off. For a moment I thought she wasn't going to come, but then the back door opened and Ricky appeared on the steps, holding a candle. She walked slowly across the lawn so as not to extinguish the flame. Its soft flickering light bathed her face. She appeared as though she were taking part in a religious procession. She had taken off her dress and was wearing a man's dressing gown — it must have been Ricky's. I remembered her wearing Uncle Roderick's dressing gown, and how I reached inside to palm her breast, how warm and good and whole it had felt.

She opened the screen door and put the candle on the table,

next to the Victrola. Then she sat across the little room from me, on the opposite bench, so the table and the candle and the Victrola were between us.

"Thank you," I said, and I think she could tell by the tone of my voice that I meant it.

She folded her arms across her breast and then collected the lapels of the gown with one hand at her throat.

"Is that Ricky's?" I asked.

"What?" Her voice was dark and soft, and it occurred to me that she might have been crying while inside.

"The dressing gown," I said.

She looked down at it. "Yes," she said. "Originally. But it's become more mine than his. And now, I suppose, it is mine completely."

"Do you miss him?" I asked. Her face was in gloom. The candle lit only the macabre face of the Victrola. Its faux-tortoiseshell horn glowed.

"Yes," she said. "I miss him terribly."

"I'm sorry," I said.

"Why?" she asked. "You've done your part in helping me forget him."

"That isn't what I thought I was doing."

"What did you think you were doing?"

"Loving you. Or trying to. Hoping to."

"And failing?"

"Yes, I suppose."

"I wish you better luck with Miss Quay."

I said nothing.

After a moment she continued. Her voice had a dark, hysterical edge to it. "Do you know, it's not here I was happiest. No, not in the summerhouse. It was in your bed. Naked in that fantastic bed of yours, in the hot afternoon, fucking with the doors and windows open. That's when I was most happy. It's funny, isn't it, that you can get the greatest physical pleasure from someone whom you don't really love. It's an odd joy, that. Odd and meaningless."

We sat for a moment or two in silence. Then she stood and blew out the candle. "Will you go now?" she asked.

I stood up. We looked at one another across the table. "You are an awful man," she said to me. Her voice had changed. She now sounded tired and calm. "You pretend to be decent. It is one of the worst deceptions that exists. You enter into relations as if you were a man of honor, when you know you are not."

"I never intended to hurt you in any way," I said. "I don't think I am as bad a person as you are making me out to be."

"I'm glad you think that," she said. "It must be a comfort to you."

"Besides," I said, "I am not myself."

"Then who are you?"

"I don't know. My life has turned me into someone who is not myself."

"All our lives do that," she said. "You think you are unique? Do you think losing my son and my husband hasn't altered me?"

"You don't understand."

"On the contrary, I understand you all too well. It begins to exhaust me, how well I understand you."

"Then I would think you might love me a little," I said.

"Why? Do you think to know you is to love you?"

"No," I said. "I only hoped . . ."

"What? What did you hope?"

"Nothing," I said. "I hoped nothing." I opened the screen door and walked across the lawn, past the birdbath, around the house. This time I did not still the little bell: I let it peal, announcing my exit.

The next morning I wrote two letters. The first was to Mr. Dent, which I sent to him care of American Express in Barcelona:

Dear Ricky,

I hope this letter finds you, and finds you well.

This is a difficult letter for me to write, and it may be inappropriate as well. But I feel compelled to let you know that your wife loves you very much and misses you terribly. She has told me so herself. And since you told me similar things when we met at Encampo that dreary night, I thought you should be apprised of your wife's feelings. Perhaps you do know them, but it seems to me that you are both dissembling, trying to do what you think is right for the other person, which only hurts you both. Perhaps you have found a life in Barcelona that pleases you, but if you have not, and if my instincts concerning you and Ricky are correct, I think you should return to her, or at least be in touch.

It would be dishonest of me not to mention in this letter the fact that I have been having an affair with Ricky practically since the time you left Andorra. I wish to make neither excuses nor apologies for my behavior, only admit to it. So please believe me when I tell you, just as honestly, that our affair is over. Ricky is disenchanted with me, and I think I flatter myself to express her feelings in those terms. But I still regard you both with great affection and that is why I take the liberty of writing you this presumptuous letter that I hope will cause some good to spring between you.

Please, for the sake of your love, write to her. And please accept my apologies if I have failed or hurt you in any way.

Yours,

The second note was much shorter, and read as follows:

Dear Mrs. Quay,

I cannot tell you how delighted I am with your kind invitation. The trip you propose sounds wonderful, and exactly what my dejected spirits require. I accept your invitation most gratefully and enthusiastically.

Yours,

PART THREE

THE SPLENDORA

*. . . small countries make de-
lightful prisons.*
—JAMES MERRILL, *The (Diblos)
Notebook*

*What more is there to do, except
stay? And that we cannot do.*
—JOHN ASHBERY, *"The Instruction
Manual"*

O<small>N THE EVENING OF THE DAY THE FALLOWFIELDS ARRIVED IN</small> Andorra from Formentera, I was invited to a dinner party at Quayside. Nothing formal, Mrs. Quay wrote—just a quiet supper whereupon acquaintances could be made.

When I arrived I was shown by Briggs, the ancient and often inactive butler, to the loggia, which was deserted. It was a warm, still evening. I wandered out across the perfectly tended lawn toward the cliff. Down below, on the little rocky beach, I could see Mrs. Quay's overturned kayak and what looked like Jean sitting on a canvas sling-back beach chair, gazing out at the water. I started down the steps, and as I neared the bottom, the figure in the chair turned away from the water and looked up at me, and I realized I was wrong: it was Nancy Quay, and as soon as I realized this, I paused for a moment, for I wasn't sure I wanted to visit with her. Nancy made me nervous. But it would have looked impolite and foolish to turn around, so I descended the rest of the way to the beach. How much of my life has been like that: proceeding only because I have passed the point where turning back was an option.

"Good evening," I said.

"Good evening," said Nancy. She was dressed casually in a pair of white calf-length pants and a blue-and-white-striped man's shirt, whose tails were knotted at her waist, exposing an inch of her tanned midriff. Her feet were bare, and I noticed her toenails were painted red. From one of her pant pockets she withdrew a cigarette case, which she opened before me. "If you're going to stand down here at this time of day, I'm afraid you'll have to smoke. Otherwise the insects will eat you alive."

I could feel them hovering unpleasantly about my face, so I reached down and took a cigarette, and then patted my pockets, as if searching out a lighter. I knew I didn't have one, but it seemed the appropriate gesture to make. I felt a little as if I were a bad actor in a play.

"Let me," she said. She slid a slim lighter out from the case, ignited it, and held it toward me. I leaned down with the cigarette in my mouth and introduced its tip to the flame. I thought about touching her hand, but did not. I inhaled, then stood up straight and exhaled a cloud of smoke at the tiny insects all around me.

"I saw you the other night," Nancy was saying. "At the cantina. You looked adorable eating that ice cream. Like a guilty little boy. You should have joined us. Or at least come to say hello."

"I'm sorry," I said. "To tell you the truth, I'm a little scared of the crowd at the cantina. It seems like such a club."

"Oh, it's nothing of the sort. In fact, it's the one spot in this awful country where people don't stand on ceremony. You should have come over. I would have introduced you 'round. Everyone thinks you're so mysterious and glamorous." She said this in a way that clearly precluded herself.

"Then I was right to stay away," I said. "I would only have disappointed them."

"Do you mean you are not as interesting as rumors suggest?"

"I very much doubt it. What are the rumors?"

"Well, our tax and extradition laws being what they are, it is assumed you are in our midst because you either made a fortune in some dubious way or murdered somebody. Of course, you could have done both, as I am told the two often coincide."

"I am afraid I have done neither."

"How disappointing! I was sure you were fleeing from something sensational. However, it's not what you've done that most interests me. It's what you're doing."

"What do you mean, what I'm doing?"

"I mean what you're doing with my sister. I'm fond of Jean—we're quite close, believe it or not—and I don't like to see men taking advantage of her."

"Do you think I have?"

"I know you have. She told me you kissed her that night. The first night you met her. Now, I know a kiss is nothing, and I'm sure it meant less than nothing to you, but you have to realize that, well, Jean takes these things seriously. She's had a very bad time of it with men. And she arrived home that night all gushing and transformed. Of course, she tried to hide it, but she couldn't. It was a little pathetic. I just wish you'd leave her alone if you're not interested."

"Who says I'm not interested?"

"Well, if you are interested, why are you so often seen with that awful Australian woman?"

"What do you mean?"

"You are the stupidest man I have ever spoken with. Is she your mistress?"

"I didn't think men had mistresses anymore."

"Men will always have mistresses, alas and alack. Or is it alack and alas?"

"Why?"

"Why what?"

"Why alas and alack?"

"Don't change the subject. What is your relation to the woman with the large dog?"

"Mrs. Dent is my friend. Was my friend."

"What do you mean, was? Do you sleep with her?"

"Isn't that a rude question?"

"Yes. But I am a rude person. And I don't understand how you can pretend to be interested in Jean when you are sleeping with another woman."

"Has it been your experience that one's interests are always perfectly exclusive?"

"You're really an awful man, aren't you?"

I said nothing.

"What a shame," she said. "I hoped, for Jean's sake, that you weren't."

"I'm trying to be a better person," I said.

"Try harder."

"In fact, my affair with Mrs. Dent is over."

"Is that a result of your self-improvement plan?"

"No," I said. "It is a result of Mrs. Dent's."

"Then she is a smarter woman than I thought."

"She is a very smart woman," I said.

"Then you agree she is well rid of you?"

"Yes," I said. "Any woman would be."

"Oh come. Don't try to make yourself irresistible." Nancy flicked her cigarette butt at the water's edge and stood up. She lit another cigarette and sat on the bottom step of the stairs. "Come sit down," she said. "Stop pacing about."

I sat next to her and watched her smoke. I liked how she did it: a little greedily, narrowing her green eyes and sucking in her cheeks, as if smoking were very hard work. And she knew how to hold a cigarette naturally and elegantly, as if it were an extension of her hand. She had beautiful hands with long, tapered fingers, but her nails, I noticed, were badly chewed.

"What did you mean about Jean? When you said before that she was unlucky with men?"

"I meant what I said."

"Who was she in love with?"

"Now it is you who are asking rude questions."

"I answered yours," I said.

She looked over at me. "It doesn't matter who it was," she said. "The point is, it made her very unhappy. And I wish you wouldn't hurt her."

"I have no intention of hurting her," I said.

"It doesn't require intent. Just be careful with Jean, that's all I ask. And now I suppose you should go up. Aren't you here to meet the gorgon?"

"Do you mean Mrs. Fallowfield?"

"Yes."

"Are you coming on the cruise?" I asked.

"No," said Nancy. "I'm taking Barbara to Scotland to see her grandmama. Another gorgon. The world is full of them, it seems."

"I wish you were coming," I said.

"Why?" she asked.

"It might be more fun," I said.

She laughed. "If it's fun you're after, I wouldn't go on the cruise."

I couldn't think how to reply to this comment without sounding disingenuous, so I said nothing. Nancy exhaled a plume of smoke and watched it drift into the evening air. We were sitting quite close together on the narrow stair and I could feel the heat from her body and smell her warm, peppery skin.

I stood and looked down at her. I put my hands in my trouser pockets, and held the material away from my legs, as I had the tentative stirrings of an erection. "Do you really think I'm an awful man?" I asked.

She looked me over, and despite my precaution, I believe she discerned my interest in her. "You have every indication of being one," she said.

"Perhaps I'll surprise you," I said.

"Please do," said Nancy.

As I climbed up over the crest of the cliff I could see the party assembled on the loggia: Mrs. Quay and Jean and two strangers, presumably the Fallowfields. I heard Mrs. Quay's rather unpleasant braying laughter. For a moment I thought about ditching it, them — my conversation with Nancy had slightly shifted my perspective, altered my palate, and I subsequently found the world of Quayside disagreeable—but, as before with Nancy, there was no way to escape without being seen, so I walked briskly across the lawn and stepped up onto the terra-cotta-tiled floor.

"There you are," said Mrs. Quay. "We thought you had blown away."

"I just went down to the beach for a moment," I said.

"Very good, very good," said Mrs. Quay, as if I were an idiot. "Well, I am so very happy to introduce you to my dear friend Isolta Fallowfield. And this is her son, Vere."

I shook both their hands. Mrs. Fallowfield had that eerily sustained tight beauty of women who have used too much of their money to retard the aging process, but there was no doubt that she had been, and perhaps still was, a beauty. Everything about her was perfect: her hair, her tucked face, her glittering eyes, her tailored suit, her slender legs, her daintily crossed ankles. She offered me her manicured hand horizontally rather than vertically, as if she expected it to be kissed. I gave it a limp little shake, genuflecting somewhat over it, resisting the urge to click my heels. Her son was quite young, and good-looking, in a foppish, overbred kind of way. He had long, flowing, jet-black hair and a holy, medieval face. His pale-blue eyes were almost preternaturally large, and his long, thin nose unfurled itself elegantly down his face like something precious made of porcelain. As I shook his huge, thin hand he said his name, Vere, out loud, and I said my name, Alex.

Then I rather stupidly shook Jean's hand. And then I sat down.

"We're drinking Lillets!" exclaimed Mrs. Quay. "But there's gin if you'd rather that."

"A Lillet will be fine," I said.

She rang a little silver bell that stood on the cocktail tray. We all waited silently for the bell to have effect, and when it became apparent that it would not, Jean stood up and said, "I'll go see if I can find Briggs." She walked through the open French doors into the salon.

I turned to Mrs. Fallowfield. "I'm grateful for your invitation," I said. "It's so kind of you to include me on your voyage."

"Think nothing of it," she said. "We're so glad you can join us. It will be nice for Vere to have a man along. Won't it, darling?"

"Yes," said Vere unenthusiastically. He looked at me strangely, as if I might not really be a man.

"Sophonsobia tells me you're American," said Mrs. Fallowfield.

"That's correct," I said. "I just recently moved to Andorra."

"My mother was American. She was a Boston Higginbottom. It's from her I get my red hair. Are you from Boston?"

"No," I said.

"What a shame," she said. "Where are you from?"

"I most recently lived in San Francisco." Jean returned with my drink. I was trying to find Mrs. Fallowfield amusing; I thought this would be in my best interest. I wondered how big her yacht was. I hoped it wasn't some tiny thing in which we would all be crammed together with the rain beating down outside.

"I understand you've been in Formentera," I said.

"Yes," she said. "Do you know the island?"

"No," I said. "But some friends of mine just came back from Ibiza."

"Poor them! I'm afraid Ibiza is ruined. Although I haven't been there in years. Perhaps it's been unruined. That can happen to places, but it takes a while. You see, a place is found, and then it's lovely for a while, and then it's ruined, and then if you're lucky it's forgotten, and if it hasn't become too, too ruined, it can start again — unruin itself. It's what's going to happen to the planet eventually, I'm sure. It's only natural and we shouldn't resist it. We'll ruin it with concrete and garbage and hairspray and blow ourselves up, and it will all lie fallow for a millennium or two, and then it will start all over again, the fish crawling out of the sea and eventually painting the Sistine Chapel. Mark my words."

After a dinner dominated by the inexhaustibly garrulous Mrs. Fallowfield, Mrs. Quay announced that the women would leave the men to smoke in the dining room. Immediately after the ladies departed the room, Briggs appeared with a box of cigars; I declined, but Vere took one and made a great show of preparing it to be smoked, as if it were a little wild animal he had just caught that required cleaning and trussing. I almost expected it to fight back. Finally the cigar was sufficiently mutilated and subdued, and he set it on fire, which involved a lot of huffing and puffing. We were sitting at opposite ends of an absurdly long table; I had thought that after the ladies left, one of us might get up and move toward the other, but apparently some territorial male pride immobilized us both. So I sat at one end drinking my brandy and he sat at the other smoking his cigar. A grotesque epergne crouched in the middle of the table, effectively blocking our view of one another. Vere pushed his chair back from the table and stretched his long borzoi legs out in front of him. Then, after a moment, he stood up and

looked out the French door, which was closed against the dark
night. I could tell he was working up his nerve to ask me something. After a long moment he turned to me.

"I don't think you remember me," he said. He wore an odd,
challenging smile.

I looked at him. He did seem vaguely familiar, but I thought it
was only his type, which he so perfectly exemplified, that I recognized. "No," I said. "Have we met before?"

"Yes," he said. "I was at your wedding."

My wedding, I thought. And then I thought: No, it's impossible.
"My wedding?" I said.

"Yes. Didn't you marry Helen Arkady?"

"Yes," I said, "but I don't remember you."

"I was a friend of your wife's brother. Philip. More than a friend,
oh so much more than a friend, in fact." He paused for a moment
and looked sentimental. I had never realized that Philip was queer.
I did not know him well, but it was nevertheless hard to reconcile:
he was now married, had two dreadful children, and lived in one
of those pretentious suburbs of Philadelphia with absurd vowel-less
Welsh names. Of course I had had nothing to do with him since
Helen had died.

"It was a lovely wedding," Vere was saying. "I remember it so
well. One of those Technicolor autumn days you see pictured on
calendars. I danced with your wife. She was so beautiful. With
flowers in her hair."

"Are you still in touch with Philip?" I asked.

"No," he said. "Philip renounced me and our debauched life-
style. I haven't spoken to him in years."

I wondered if this was really true. "You're well rid of him," I said. "He's become a very dreary man. But how did you come to know Philip?"

Vere sat down at the place beside me. "I met him at Cambridge. He was on a Rhodes scholarship, studying history. He had the most marvelously formed ears I've ever seen. And he always carried a satchel with a racket sticking out of it, which I found very arousing. I'm afraid I rather shamelessly pounced on him."

"And you came back to the States with him?"

"Yes, but it didn't last. Apparently his interest in me was site-specific. But I had a very happy time with him at your wedding. What a golden day. And how is your wife?"

The aromatic blue smoke of his cigar drifted my way, and I coughed a little into my fist.

"I'm sorry," he said. He waved at the smoke with his hand, which only succeeded in diffusing it more generally.

"I'm afraid my wife is dead," I said.

"Christ," said Vere. "I'm so sorry. I had no idea—"

"No," I said. "Of course you did not."

"Well, I'm very sorry," said Vere. "Did she die recently?"

"About a year ago," I said.

"It's hard to fathom," he said. "I mean, only having seen her at your wedding, so beautiful and young and happy. When you see people like that you assume their life will go on and on. How awful life can be."

"Yes," I said.

We sat for a moment, awkwardly silent. I felt ill. Perhaps it was the cigar smoke, or perhaps it was the cold poached salmon with

Nile-green sauce which had not acclimated itself happily to life in my stomach.

"I suppose we should go and join the ladies," Vere finally said.

I stood. "Actually," I said, "I'm not feeling well. I wonder if you'll make my excuses for me. I think I'll head home."

Vere put out his cigar and stood up. "I'm so sorry. I hope I haven't upset you."

"No," I said. "I think it was the salmon."

"Can I get you some tea? Or something fizzy to drink?"

"No," I said. "I think I'll be more comfortable just going home. Will you say good night for me?"

"Certainly, if that's what you want. Perhaps the fresh air will do you good. Now that you mention it, the salmon did seem a bit off. I do hope you feel better."

I held out my hand and he shook it. We said good night, and I opened the French door and stepped out onto the flagstone terrace. I could see Mrs. Quay's archery target set at the edge of the lawn, and I walked toward it, out of the halo of light the great house cast. I carefully walked down the steps to the beach. I sat down in the canvas chair Nancy had left behind and looked out at the water, taking deep breaths, trying to calm myself. So he had touched Helen. He had danced with her in the golden afternoon.

The huge sky seemed ridiculously full of stars, and the glittering commotion of it made me feel sicker. I closed my eyes. It was leaves, not flowers, that Helen had worn in her hair. Autumn leaves. A parched crown. We were married out-of-doors, at her grandparents' huge clapboard house in western Massachusetts. They were White Russians, her grandparents, Boris and Ylena, and there was about their house the feeling of a dacha. Dampness in the air and a low thin mist. I remember I stood and watched Helen emerge from the house and trek across the lawn toward the party assembled at the far edge of the meadow. We all turned and watched her. She came by herself. She did not want anyone to give her away. And she seemed to take forever, walking through the tall grass, and as she got closer we could see she was smiling yet crying in a sort of radiant way, and she had her eyes fixed on me, she did not look down or around but straight at me; it was me she walked toward, me she came to across that great silent distance, with tears in her eyes and leaves in her hair, as if I were a safe place she might lose sight of if she glanced, even briefly, away.

CHAPTER EIGHTEEN

I SLEPT LATE THE NEXT MORNING AND AWOKE FEELING WEAK and disoriented. I was lying in bed, gazing up at the clutched wooden hands above me, trying to talk myself back into being myself, when I heard a voice calling me from downstairs. It sounded like Miss Quay's.

I got out of bed and stood at the top of the stairs. "Hello?" I called.

"Alex? It's Jean Quay. I've come to see how you're feeling. May I come up?"

"I'll be right down," I said. I hurriedly washed my face and put on some clothes. Miss Quay was standing apprehensively in the center of the dim living room, as if she thought the furniture might attack her. "I hope I'm not dragging you from your sickbed," she said as I entered the room.

"Not at all," I said. "I'm feeling much better."

"Good," she said. "Everyone at Quayside is concerned. Vere said you turned the strangest color. You still look quite pale. Why don't you sit down. May I make you some tea? If I'm not mistaken, Uncle Roddy has some ginger tea in the cupboard. It will soothe your stomach."

"That sounds perfect," I said.

"Then sit down, and I will make a pot."

I sat on the couch and watched Miss Quay disappear into the kitchen. After a moment I stood up and pulled back the drapes, opened the doors to the terrace, and stepped outside. I looked over the wall, down at the activity in the street: Ali was supervising the unloading of burlap sacks from a team of burros that stood patiently on the cobblestones. I turned around when I heard Miss Quay call my name. She stood in the doorway, holding a rattan tray with tea paraphernalia. "It's too hot and bright for you out there," she said. "It's much cooler in here. Come indoors."

I followed her back into the living room. She laid the tray on a low table and sat on the couch, and I sat beside her, watching her pour the tea through a strainer into two small handleless cups. They were the cups Ricky had used as an ashtray. Miss Quay handed me one and said, "Drink this."

I sipped the tea. It was very hot and had an intense, peculiar flavor.

Miss Quay watched me sip my tea for a moment and then sipped her own. "People always think that in hot weather they should drink cold beverages, but it isn't true," she said. "A hot drink actually reduces one's internal temperature more quickly. I learned that in Ceylon."

I knew some sort of polite reply was expected, but my grogginess made me incapable of small talk. Large sections of my brain seemed turned off, shrouded, yet visions of my encounter with Miss Quay in the War Memorial Garden kept appearing at the edges of my consciousness, like some fleeting but reoccurring moment artfully spliced over and over again into an avant-garde film, and I did not know how to reconcile these visions with the fact of Miss Quay and me sitting together now on the sofa, quietly sipping tea.

"When were you in Ceylon?" I finally, and unbrilliantly, managed.

"Oh," she said, "about ten years ago. I went out there to live with my aunt and uncle."

Our little conversation seemed to have climbed down the rungs of a ladder and disappeared. After a moment of silence Miss Quay placed her cup of tea on the tray and said, "Are you feeling any better?"

"Yes," I said. "Thank you."

She lifted the teapot. "Would you like some more?"

"No, thank you," I said.

She returned the pot to the tray and looked at it sadly, as if I had snubbed it. Or no: it was as if everything, even the pot of tea, finally disappointed her. She reached out and touched it, ostensibly, I suppose, to discern its temperature, but there was in her gesture an almost pathetic tenderness, as if the warm ceramic skin of the teapot afforded her the only comfort she would ever know. After a moment she withdrew her hand, stood and picked up the tray, and carried it into the kitchen. I sat for a moment, finishing my tea, and then I followed her.

She was rinsing the pot out beneath the tap. The water crashed into the top of the pot and then erupted, in a thin bright stream, from its spout. I handed her my cup and she rinsed that. Then she turned off the water and wiped her hands on a small towel.

"I owe you an apology," I said.

She hung the towel over the neck of the faucet, carefully balancing the two drooping wings of it, and looked at me. "Oh dear," she said. "What about?"

"My behavior in the War Memorial Garden. I'm sorry if it was inappropriate."

"It is never inappropriate to be human," said Miss Quay. "On the contrary, I think that if we all broke down and wept once in a while, the world would be a better place."

"Why?"

"Because we wouldn't spend so much energy resisting and hiding the sadness that is inside us. We would admit it, share it. As you did." She looked down at the floor, and moved her shoe, appraisingly, across the grimy tiles. "And as I did, that first night we came here."

I said nothing, wondering if she would go on.

"Why did you cry then?" I asked, when she did not.

She looked up, a little abruptly and, I thought, angrily. "Why?" But when her eyes met mine the anger faded, settled, and she said, "I cried because I was sad. Being here, in Uncle Roddy's house, made me think of Ceylon—I suppose because that is where he has gone to, and . . . that made me sad."

"Why?"

She smiled her sad smile, and shook her head. "Because my heart was broken in Ceylon. Do people still say that? I remember that is how it felt. I was miserable. And remembering it, even now, at this great distance, makes me sad."

"What happened?" I asked.

She turned the tap back on and rinsed her hands with the cold water, as if she could not continue without cold, clean hands. She shook them into the sink and then wiped them with the towel.

"Please tell me what happened," I said.

She repositioned the towel and leaned back against the counter so that she was facing me. She looked at me for a moment, quizzically, judging me.

"It was nothing so unusual," she said. "Or even secret, although of course we never speak of it. Like the death of my brother. I don't understand why the things that hurt us the most are the things we remain silent about." She paused, as if I might have an explanation, but when she saw I did not, she continued. "I went to Ceylon when I was twenty-eight. Although it was never stated, I knew that Mother sent me there to find a husband. You see, I had not found one here, and I was getting old. I suppose Mother thought it might be easier for me in Ceylon, the competition would be less keen. I was not a pretty girl. I was too tall, you see, and large—and, well, shy and awkward. So I was sent to live with my Aunt Charlotte and Uncle Demerest at Massiliwawood, their teak plantation. And I did fall in love, almost immediately, terribly and wonderfully in love. Although not with one of those beefy uncouth British boys—the detritus of the Empire—that Aunt Charlotte constantly invited to dinner. I fell in love with someone unsuitable: a native. He was the foreman on the plantation. He was the kindest and most beautiful man I have ever known. Ever. And the smartest, as well. Certainly the best-read. You see, he snuck into the house late at night to borrow books from my uncle's library—books my uncle never read, beautiful leather-bound books shipped halfway around the world moldering in the heat with their pages still unopened. He was reading every book in the room, all the Greeks, all of Shakespeare and Dickens, Austen and Ruskin and Zola and Tolstoy; he snuck in and took one book at a go. That is how I met him: late at night, in the library. And oh— He was so kind and so beautiful. So good. So totally good." She paused for moment, remembering. "I knew it was unacceptable to people like Aunt Charlotte and my mother. I knew he would not be thought a proper husband. So I kept it a secret. I snuck out at night to his little cottage and came back to the big house at dawn, so happy, so unbelievably happy. No: believably happy; you must believe in happiness like that. You must." She exhaled a long, shaky breath. "When I knew I was pregnant I told my aunt and uncle that I would marry him. I knew I would have to insist, and so I did. I insisted I would marry him.

"They acted so quickly, so cruelly. I never saw him again. I was locked in my room. The next day I was put on the train to Colombo. From there I traveled by ship to a convent in Ireland. It was as far away from him as they could think to put me."

"What happened then?" I asked.

"I stayed there until the baby was born," she said. "I know it was a boy, but they told me he died on his second day. I think they were lying. I think they thought it would be easier for me if I thought our baby was dead. Maybe not. I can't know. Would nuns lie about something like that?"

"I don't know," I said.

"After that I went to London. For about six months I worked as a secretary for an ophthalmologist. But I was lonely there, and miserable. It always seemed to be raining. And his windowless office, with the eye charts and corrective lenses. And so I came back to Andorra."

"And you never tried to be in touch with him?"

"How could I? The only way was through my aunt and uncle. And besides, I am sure they sent him away. Or did something worse. People are so cruel, even about love. Especially about love, it seems. I thought I might hear from him, somehow—it's one of the reasons why I came back to Andorra, I thought he might try to contact me here, but he never has.

"It was my fault you see, telling my aunt. It was so stupid and naïve of me. To think they would allow me to marry him. He knew better. He wanted me to go away with him, but I would not do that. I am the one who decided to tell Aunt and Uncle. And so I lost my chance with him."

"You may still hear from him," I said. "One day."

"No," she said. "I don't even wish for that anymore. You can't— it's bad for you, it hurts you, to wish stupidly like that. I lost my chance with him, and I accept that now."

"It is a very sad story," I said. "I'm sorry."

She looked at me. "I'm glad I told you," she said. Then she stood up straight. "Well. I must return to Quayside. I promised Bitsy I would be home for lunch. She leaves for Scotland this evening. Oh, and I am instructed by Isolta to tell you to make sure you remember to bring your passport with you tomorrow. You will need it to enter all foreign ports."

She pushed open the kitchen door and walked across the living room. I followed her and opened the outside door. She stepped onto the stoop and then turned around. "I'm looking forward to the cruise," she said. "I'm so glad you're coming."

"Yes," I said. "So am I."

"Well," she said. "I'll see you tomorrow, then. We plan to sail about noon, so you'll want to be at the marina sometime before then. We'll send someone for your bags in the morning. We won't be dressing for dinner, so there's no need to pack anything formal. I suppose it might get cool at night, so make sure you have something warm. What else? The boat's the *Splendora*. I'm sure it will be the biggest boat there. You can't miss it. Don't forget your passport." And then she turned and quickly descended the steps and disappeared into the alley.

It wasn't until I got upstairs and was rooting through Uncle Roderick's desk for my passport that I remembered it had been requisitioned weeks ago by Lieutenant Afgroni and never returned. Presumably it was still at the police station. I sat there wondering what to do. Could I go on the cruise without the passport? Pretend I had forgotten it? But it would look stupid to arrive without the one thing I had been instructed to bring. No: I would have to reclaim it. After all, there was no reason for me not to have it, or the Andorran authorities to be holding it. I was sure I remembered Afgroni saying they would keep it for a few days only. It was probably waiting to be repossessed.

And so I hastened in the midday heat, still feeling a little woozy, to the municipal building. I paused in the rotunda to study the directory; I wanted to avoid the police if possible. It listed an office

of RECORDS, LICENSES & PASSPORTS on the second floor, and I
decided to start there. I climbed the stairs and walked down a long,
deserted hall. The room I entered was small, entirely paneled in
wood, and illuminated by a few alabaster globes that hung from
the ceiling. It was dark and hushed in a way that made it impossible
to believe that the bright day still existed beyond the walls. Directly
in front of me an ornate iron grille rose up to the ceiling from an
intricately carved wooden counter that bisected the room. The dim
light, the dark wood, and the iron grille all gave the small room
the aura of the confessional.

"How may I help you?" An elderly woman materialized, like an
absolutionist, in the gloom behind an opening in the grille. She
was dressed in an odd black-and-white costume that made her look
like a cross between a nun and an usherette.

"I'm here to inquire about my passport," I said, stepping toward
the counter. "I believe you may be holding it here for me to pick
up."

"What makes you believe that?" the woman said. She looked
beyond me and addressed herself to the air above my head.

"Well, I had given it to the police some time ago."

"The police!" She raised her voice, almost as if summoning
them.

"Yes," I said. "The police requested my passport for a day or two
quite some time ago and it has yet to be returned to me. I thought
it might be waiting for me here."

"The Clerk's Office does not involve itself with criminal matters," said the woman. "You must see the police about your pass-

port. They are located on the subterranean level." She ever so slightly stressed the word subterranean, as if the direction in which I must proceed was somehow indicative of my character. "Good day," she said. She reached up and lowered a brown paper shade between us, but I could tell she remained in place.

For a moment we stood on either side of the shade, and then I said, "It is not a criminal matter."

She made no response. I could tell she was standing perfectly still, in an effort to convince me that she was no longer there. I knocked three times with my knuckles on the counter. I could sense her step back, slightly, and I knocked again, this time a little more forcefully.

"What do you want?" she asked.

"I want you to look at me," I said.

She peeled back an edge of the paper shade and peered at me.

"I am not a criminal," I said.

She shrugged. "I never said you were."

"You implied that I was."

"I made no estimation of your character whatsoever. I simply directed you to the police. Your passport is not here and I can help you no more." She let go of the shade.

I went downstairs.

The police area was all fluorescent light and Formica, the exact opposite of the Office of Records, Licenses & Passports. I was shown to a desk behind which an officer sat.

"I am here to reclaim my passport," I said.

"Lost and found is upstairs in the cloakroom," he said.

"I have not lost my passport. It was taken from me, by the police, several weeks ago, and I was told I could reclaim it after a few days. I am here to do that."

"Certainly," he said. "You need only fill out this form." He rummaged in a drawer and gave me a form titled RECLAMATION OF CONFISCATED/QUARANTINED ITEMS. It required my name, address, the item to be reclaimed, its estimated value, and the reason why it was confiscated. At the bottom of the form was the following disclaimer: *All foodstuffs and unlicensed livestock are destroyed after forty-eight hours.*

I returned the completed form to the adjutant. I realized I had never seen any of these theatrically costumed policemen on the streets of Andorra; in fact, I had seen no police at all; they seemed to exist only in the subterranean level of the municipal building.

He glanced at the form and then stood. "I will return," he told me. I watched him disappear through a door, and I waited only moments before he reappeared. He stood beside the desk, cleared his throat, and said, "If you will please follow me."

I was about to obey him, but then I thought better of it. I remained seated. "If I will follow you, what?" I asked.

"Sir?"

"It is an incomplete sentence: if you will please follow me. Please complete it. What will happen if I follow you? Will I get my passport? Will I be executed? IF I FOLLOW YOU, WHAT?"

The police officer took a step away from me, as if I were a dangerous lunatic. I waited patiently, but instead of answering my question he merely reformulated his own: "Please follow me."

I got up and followed him, out the door, down the long hall, past the MORTUAIRE and into a little private office like the one in which I had been interrogated by Lieutenant Afgroni. In fact, it could have been the same office. "Someone will be with you in a moment," he said, and closed the door. I could tell he was relieved to be done with me. By this point I felt somewhat defeated, and I cursed myself for ever giving my passport up in the first place. I should never have let it be taken from me. How stupid! In the future I would be less cooperative, the future being now.

The door opened and Lieutenant Afgroni entered the room, closing it behind him. He was once again elegantly dressed in a suit; his thick hair was brilliantined, his nails manicured. How I hated him. He sat down at the desk and pretended to study my reclamation form for a moment before looking up at me. "Ah, Mr. Fox," he said. "So we meet again."

"Good afternoon," I said.

"I see you have come for your passport," he said. He laid the form in the center of the empty desktop.

"Yes," I said. "I should like to have it back immediately."

"Immediately!" He chuckled. "Why the great rush? Are you planning a trip?"

"As a matter of fact, I am," I said. "I leave tomorrow."

"May I ask where you intend to go?"

"You may not," I said. I was determined not to be diverted from my sole purpose. "I don't see how the personal travel plans of an American citizen concern you in the least."

"On the contrary, in your case they concern me a great deal."

"I don't see why they should," I said.

Lieutenant Afgroni, who had been leaning forward, settled back into his chair. He stroked the skin above his upper lip, giving me the impression he had once had a mustache that he now missed. He raised his eyebrows. "I can't say that I admire your attitude," he said.

"And I can't say that I care." I stood up. "If you do not intend to give me my passport, please tell me so, and I will take the matter up with the United States Embassy."

"That will be difficult for you to do," he said, "since there is no United States Embassy in Andorra."

"Then I will speak to the consul. There must be some office of the United States government in La Plata."

Lieutenant Afgroni shook his head. "Alas, there is none. I am afraid we are too small and unimportant a country to be recognized in any official way by the United States."

"Then I will go to Paris," I said, "and take the matter up there."

"You will need your passport to get to Paris," said Lieutenant Afgroni. "I remember that you like brandy. Would you like one now?"

"I would not," I said.

"Well, please sit down."

"I prefer to stand," I said. "Actually, I prefer not to be here at all. I will pursue the matter of my purloined passport through other channels. Excuse me."

"Before you embarrass yourself any further, Mr. Fox, I should tell you that I am afraid I am the only 'channel' through which you can presently pursue the matter of your passport. In fact, I have it here, with me." He took it out of his breast pocket and tossed it on the desk. "Now please sit down. I have, as you no doubt expect, a few questions to ask you."

I stood for a moment, as if I was considering my options, and then sat down. I looked at him.

He smiled at me. "Thank you," he said. "May I repeat my offer of a brandy?"

"You may," I said. "But I would once again refuse it."

"Then it does not bear repeating."

He picked up my passport and glanced through it, flipping the pages, turning it sideways to read the different stamps. There was a certain theatrical artificiality about everything he did that infuriated me. "Where did you stay your first night in Andorra?"

"At the Hotel Excelsior," I said.

"Are you sure?"

"Of course I am sure," I said. "You can check their records if you don't believe me."

"We have. They show that you arrived on Monday, the seventeenth of May."

"That is correct," I said.

"Then where did you stay the night of the sixteenth of May?"

"Nowhere. I was en route from Paris. I took the overnight train."

"So you have said. At what time did you arrive?"

"I don't remember exactly. Early. About eight, I think."

"The night train usually arrives at six. Do you remember if it was delayed that morning?"

"I don't believe it was, although of course it may have been. I don't remember. In any case, what does it matter?"

"It matters a great deal. A murder was committed in La Plata on the night of May 16."

"Are you accusing me of murder?" I asked.

"Not at the present time."

"Do you plan to accuse me of murder sometime in the future?"

"It is against a policeman's nature to prognosticate."

"I should like to meet with my attorney before I answer any more of your questions. Or do your charming customs deny me that right?"

"Of course you have the right to speak with an attorney. Remember, I have accused you of nothing, Mr. Fox. I am merely asking you some questions."

"You need not explain to me what you are doing. It is obvious to me what you are doing."

"So long as we understand one another," said Lieutenant Afgroni.

"So long as we understand one another, what?" I asked. I was sick of people not finishing their sentences.

"So long as we understand one another, there can be no misunderstanding between us. I will detain you no longer."

"May I have my passport?" I asked.

"Ah, your passport," he said. He picked it up off the desk. "No. I am not at liberty to return it to you. I hope this does not prove too much of an inconvenience."

"In fact, it does," I said.

"That's right. You said you had planned a trip. I'm so sorry. But until this matter is cleared up, we would like you to remain in our country."

"And what if the matter is never cleared up?"

"I assure you it will be. Crimes don't go unsolved in Andorra."

"You mean you always find someone to blame." I stood up.

He looked at me for a moment, as if I were a tiresome child. "I meant what I said," he said.

"Am I free to go?" I asked him.

"Of course you are free to go," he said. He waved me away. "Don't overdramatize the situation."

I sought refuge and reflection in the cantina, only to find Mrs. Dent and Dino. I hadn't seen them since the night she had abandoned me — or, I suppose, I had abandoned her — in her back yard. The night of our "accident." She was sitting at the table we had occupied at our first meeting, reading a newspaper and eating her lunch. I sat at the bar and ordered a double vodka, which I consumed with a few desperate gulps. Then I went and stood beside Mrs. Dent's table.

She glanced up at me, then back at her newspaper. "Fancy meeting you here," she said.

"I need your help," I said.

"Do you?" she asked.

"Yes," I said. "This isn't funny." '

"Oh," she said, "don't worry. I don't think this is funny." She pretended she was reading her newspaper and turned a page.

"May I sit down?" I asked.

"You may," she said.

I sat down opposite her. She closed the newspaper and peered across the table at me. "You don't look at all well," she said.

"I'm not," I said.

"What's wrong?"

"Everything," I moaned.

"I doubt it," she said. "Be specific."

"I can't get my passport back from the police."

"That hardly qualifies as everything."

"And now they think I'm the one who's been murdering people and throwing their bodies in the harbor."

"Are you?" she asked me.

"Of course not," I said. "How could you even ask me that?"

"I don't know," she said. "It seems, under the circumstances, a logical question."

The waiter interrupted us to ask if I was eating. I realized I was starving. I ordered a salade fenouil, lotte meunière, and a glass of Pouilly-Fuissé.

"What am I going to do?" I asked, as the waiter departed.

"To tell you the truth, it doesn't interest me much," she said. She pretended to return her attention to the front page of the newspaper.

"Perhaps I could borrow Ricky's passport," I said. I was only thinking aloud, but it seemed a good idea. "Did he leave it behind when he fled over the mountains?"

"No."

"Are you sure?" I asked.

"I am sure. Not that I would lend it to you if he had."

"It probably wouldn't have worked anyway," I said.

"If you didn't murder the people, you have nothing to fear," Ricky said.

I remembered saying much the same thing to her husband, that cold damp morning up on the Vega. I shivered. "Of course I do. You don't understand the police."

My wine arrived and I sipped it. "Please stop reading the newspaper," I said. "It's rude."

She folded it and tossed it on the floor next to Dino. Then she looked at me. "I wouldn't want to be rude," she said.

"I'm sorry," I said.

"For what?"

"Everything," I said.

"You are too unspecific for words," she said.

"I'm sorry I decided to go on the cruise," I said.

She shrugged a little, but smiled.

"Will you help me?" I asked.

"Help you with what?"

"Think!" I said. "I can't seem to think. I need to make a plan."

"Well, what is it you want?"

"I want to get my passport back. And get these ridiculous murder charges cleared."

"They've charged you?"

"No. But they keep insinuating that I'm guilty."

"I'm sure it's just a ploy. Insinuations are harmless. Have you spoken with a lawyer?"

"No," I said.

My salad arrived, the rings of fennel artfully juxtaposed with cartwheels of hemorrhaging blood orange. I pushed it aside.

"Well, do that. Go see a lawyer: that's my advice. That should be your plan."

"Yes," I said, "I will." I paused. "But there's still the problem of the cruise."

She sighed, as if I were asking her to advise me about state affairs. "What's the problem there?"

"I can't go unless I have my passport."

"Then don't go."

"But what will I tell the Quays? That my passport is in police custody because I'm a murder suspect?"

"You're a good liar," she said. "Make something up."

"I suppose I shall have to," I said.

"Yes," she said. "You always do. And now I will leave you to eat in peace." She stood up and gathered her things. "Come, Dino," she said. They began to walk toward the door.

"Wait," I said.

She turned.

"I am sorry for everything," I said.

She paused for a moment. Dino sat down. "I believe you are sorry to the extent you can be sorry," she said.

"What does that mean?"

"It means— No. I shouldn't judge you. I believe you. If you feel sorry and say you are, then I believe you. I do."

"Thank you," I said.

She shrugged and turned to go.

"Have you heard from Ricky?" I asked.

She turned back toward me, her eyes narrowed. "How did you know?" she asked.

"Did you?" I asked.

"Yes," she said. "I did."

"What does he say?"

She paused for a minute, deciding if she would tell me. "He's fine. He's still in Barcelona. He's planning to buy a vineyard in Australia. Near Adelaide. He wants me to move there with him. He thinks we can make a go of it together."

"Do you know anything about grapes?" I asked.

"No," she said. "But I can learn."

"So you're going?"

She looked at me. "I don't know," she said. "I really don't know."

"I think you should go," I said.

"I don't care what you think," she said. She paused, and then walked back toward me. She touched my shoulder. "I'm sorry. Forgive me. I don't want to be angry with you. Or nasty. And I'm sorry for the things I said the other night. It's only that—" She shook her head. "I really don't know what to do. Or where to go. I'm so lost." She took her hand off my shoulder, and for a moment she just stood there. "I can't keep making mistakes."

"Ricky loves you," I said. "The note he had me give you was just pretending—nonsense. He thought it would help you forget him. He thought you wanted to forget him."

"Yes," she said. "He wrote me that."

"You don't, do you?"

"No," she said. "I love him."

"Then you'll go?"

"Yes," she said. "I suppose I will. Despite all our problems, I think we do belong together."

"I know you do," I said.

"I remember that first day I saw you here, at this table. I wanted to know you. I don't know why. I just did. And I'm glad I did, finally. I wish you happiness."

"And I wish you the same," I said. I stood up.

"Perhaps one of us will get lucky," she said.

We embraced. We held each other. It felt good to hold her. She was a solid person, and in a way she knew me. In a way.

And then she left the cantina, Dino padding after her in his weary, loyal fashion.

When I finished my meal I walked out to Quayside to excuse myself from the cruise. I found Mrs. Quay and Isolta Fallowfield ensconced on the loggia having tea, and Vere and Jean and Bitsy playing boccie on the lawn. I joined the old ladies in the shade. I felt tired and defeated, and it seemed where I belonged.

Mrs. Quay poured me a cup of tea. "How good to see you," she said. "And I'm so happy to hear that you've recovered. You still look a little green about the gills, I think, but the sea air will soon change that."

"Actually," I said, "I've come with some bad news."

"Oh no!" said Mrs. Quay. "What is that?"

"I'm afraid I won't be able to join you after all. I've just been to see my doctor, and apparently I'm not as well as I thought. He advised me not to go on the cruise."

"Oh, don't listen to doctors!" cried Isolta. "That is one thing I have learned. A cruise is obviously just what you need. We will return you in the pink of health."

"I am almost sure you would, but I don't want to risk anything,"

I said. "I have had some health problems lately and I need to be very careful. I thought living quietly in Andorra might cure them, but my doctor thinks if I'm not extremely careful, I may well suffer a serious relapse."

"And you look such a healthy man!" exclaimed Mrs. Quay. "How very sad. For you, and for us. We shall miss you, my dear Alex." She reached out and clasped my hand in hers. Then she leaned back in her chair, pounded her cane on the floor, and called out to the boccie players, "Jean, put down those stupid balls and come here at once. Mr. Fox has some very sad news."

Miss Quay and Vere approached the loggia. Bitsy remained behind and rearranged the balls. "Mr. Fox has just told us he cannot come on our cruise," said Mrs. Quay. "His doctor forbids it."

"Why?" asked Miss Quay. She stood in the strip of shade made by one of the columns, a little hot and flushed from the sun. She was wearing a shiftlike dress with a sailor collar. She held a boccie ball in one of her large hands.

"I had been ill before coming to Andorra," I said, "with a sort of chronic motion sickness. In fact, that is one of the reasons why I came to Andorra—I thought that living in a country this small, where one walks so much and rides so little, would have a tonic effect on my health."

"And it has not?" asked Mrs. Quay.

"It has," I said. "But my doctor thinks a sea cruise might set me back considerably. It is a risk he advised me not to take."

"I say stuff the doctor!" said Isolta. "He doesn't know the *Splendora*. It sails as smoothly as honey from a bee."

"No, no," said Mrs. Quay. "He must follow his doctor's orders. Although I thought they had medicinal patches now, for people who suffer motion sickness."

"My case is unusual and does not respond to conventional treatment," I said. "I should never have accepted your invitation in the first place, but I hoped I was sufficiently recovered to join you. I've felt so well since arriving here. And until last night I was fine. My doctor thinks the very idea of the cruise was making me ill — a sort of anticipatory pyschosomania. I can't tell you how sorry I am."

"As are we," said Mrs. Quay. "As are we."

I stood up. "Well, I'm sure you have lots of planning and packing to do, so I'll leave you now. I do hope you have a wonderful time, and look forward to hearing all about it as soon as you return."

"Oh, don't go!" said Mrs. Quay. "Surely you'll stay for dinner?"

"Thank you, but no," I said. "I should go home and rest."

"Well, it's too too sad," she said. "We shall miss you terribly."

"Thank you so much for your invitation, Mrs. Fallowfield. It was extraordinarily kind of you." I reached down and shook her hand.

"Another time, perhaps," she said. "If your health allows."

"I hope so," I said. I turned to Vere. "I enjoyed meeting you," I said. "Or seeing you again, I should say."

He shook my hand. "Yes," he said. "It was a pleasure. I'm sorry you won't be able to join us, but I'm sure we'll meet again, and I look forward to it."

"I'll walk you to the gate," said Miss Quay. She tossed the boccie ball recklessly out onto the lawn in the direction of her crouching niece.

We walked around the front of the house and up the gravel drive.

We were silent for a moment, and then Miss Quay said, "Vere told me he upset you last night. He feels so sorry about it."

"He didn't upset me," I said.

She looked at me. "Didn't he?" she asked.

"Well," I said, "maybe a little." This admission seemed to satisfy her in some way.

"Is it really your health?"

"What?"

"Is it really your health that prevents you from joining us?"

"No," I said.

"I thought not."

I said nothing.

"Is your not coming in some way connected to your conversation with Vere?"

I looked at her. Her flush had faded; she was pale and serious. "No," I said. "Of course not. Why would it?"

She bit her lip. "May I ask what it is that does prevent you from coming?"

"A silly, stupid, embarrassing complication."

"What?"

"My passport."

"It isn't current? That can be fixed."

"Oh, it's current all right. It's just not currently in my possession. The police have confiscated it."

"The police!" she said, and I remembered the sepulchral woman behind the bars in the Clerk's Office saying the same words in the same way, with alarm and distaste.

"Yes," I said. "I've been having some trouble with the police."

"What sort of trouble?"

"I'd really rather not say," I said. We had arrived at the gates, and loitered there, in the shadowed pattern of Qs they cast onto the gravel of the peninsula road.

"No," she said, "tell me. Otherwise I'll think it's something really ghastly, which I'm sure it's not."

"I'm afraid it is. Do you know about these murders? These bodies that have been found in the harbor?"

"I have read about them," she said.

"The police suspect me," I said.

"Why?"

We began to wander along the verge, in the shadow of the wall, toward the stone bench, the bench I had sat on that damp day I first visited Quayside.

"I don't really know. I told you it was ridiculous. But this one inspector has convinced himself that I'm a murderer. And he's doing his best to make things very difficult for me at the moment."

"I don't know what to say," she said. "Do you need help? I mean, what kind of help do you need?"

"It's not—I haven't been formally accused of anything yet. I'm not sure what will happen. I'm planning to see Edward Darlingham about it all, see what he thinks I should do."

"Yes, do that. Edward is brilliant and very kind. I'm sure he can help you. But nevertheless, I don't like to leave you in this terrible state. Perhaps I shan't go on the cruise."

"Don't be absurd," I said. "Of course you should go on the cruise. I'm sure I'll be fine. I just have to get out of this mess."

She looked at me, and I could tell I had hurt her.

"I'm sorry," I said. "It's very kind of you to offer to stay, but unnecessary. I will be fine. You mustn't worry. I wouldn't have told you if I thought it would worry you."

"Of course it worries me." She was angry now. "Why would I not be worried?"

"But I don't want you to worry. I want you to go, and enjoy the cruise."

"I shan't enjoy it. I shall think of you the whole time I'm gone."

We sat on the bench. For a moment we said nothing. Miss Quay was sitting in an odd twisted way, supporting her weight with one hand pressed against the lichened slab of stone. She was looking down at her hand.

I looked across the road, at the trees that lined it, the old, tall trees, the afternoon sunlight falling theatrically on their leaves. Some birds, large black birds, crows perhaps, or ravens, rose suddenly from within the trees' green nimbus like a semaphore and flew off toward La Plata. For a long time we sat there, as if we were waiting for a bus that wasn't coming.

Miss Quay—it was odd that I still thought of her, somehow, as Miss Quay—stood up. She crossed her arms and clutched them, as if she were cold. "I think you should leave Andorra," she said. She looked down at me.

"Why?" I asked.

"Nothing good will come for you here. I'm sorry, but it's true. I know something about how the police work. They'll make life unbearable for you. If they think you're guilty, they'll ruin you. I saw it happen to my father. You see, there was a scandal. It was said' he benefited more than he ought to have from the Upland Initiative. That he ruined Encampo, rebuilt it, only to line his own pockets. I don't believe it, but it's what people thought. Nothing was ever proved, but the police hounded him. They drove him to his death. And if they think you're guilty, they'll do the same to you."

"What can they do?"

"I don't know. I mean, I don't know specifically. But I know they do things to people. You'll never find peace here."

"But I can't leave," I said. "I don't have my passport."

"We can smuggle you out. Tomorrow. On the *Splendora*."

"You mean I should stow away?"

"Yes. Think about it. It's your only chance. Once you're on the boat and we're away from Andorra, we'll drop you someplace in France. And you'll be safe then."

"It sounds as though you want to get rid of me."

"I want to help you," she said. "I want to save you. I know if you stay here something terrible will happen."

"But I don't want to leave Andorra," I said. "I wanted to live here for a long time. To start a new life here. It was my dream."

"But don't you see it's not a question anymore of what you want or, worse still, dream? It's a question of what you must do. You must trust me. You must."

"I do," I said.

"Good," she said. "I must go back or they will be suspicious. But meet me tonight, at midnight, at the cantina. I suppose I will have to tell Vere, but I trust him. We'll get you on board tonight and then leave in the morning."

"What about the crew? Isn't there a crew?"

"Just the captain and a steward and a cook. They may not even be on the boat. If they are, we can deal with them. Do you have money?"

"Of course," I said. "Some."

"Well, get all the cash you can. You'll need it. I'll give you what I have."

"No," I said. "I can't take your money."

"Don't be stupid," she said. "But we can't argue about this now. I must go back. Do you understand? Tonight, midnight, in the alley beside the cantina. Don't tell anyone where you are going or what you're doing."

We walked back toward the gate, and stood just inside it.

"What did Vere tell you?" I asked.

"About what?" she asked.

"About my wife."

"He said she was very beautiful. That he danced with her at your wedding. That he was in love with her brother."

"And nothing else?"

She shook her head. "No," she said.

"There's something I should tell you," I said. "Something I want to tell you."

She silenced me by touching my arm and said, "No. Tell me later, if you must, but there isn't time now. I must get back to them." And then she turned and set off toward the house. The collar of her dress was picked up and fluttered by a sudden breeze, and the sun cast her shadow behind her, her long, thin shadow, reaching back toward me across the impossibly green lawn.

CHAPTER NINETEEN

ALI CALLED OUT TO ME AS I PASSED THE STORE ON MY WAY home. "Come here," he said.

I entered the café. He was squatting in the dark back room, transferring coffee beans from burlap sacks into large ceramic urns. It was cool and fragrant, and the sound of the beans pelting endlessly into the vessels was oddly comforting. Ali waited to speak until the canister was full. "You had a visitor," he announced.

"Who?" I asked.

"A Lieutenant Afgroni."

"What did he want?"

"You," said Ali.

"And what did you tell him?"

"I told him that he could not have you. That you were not here. He said he would return."

"When?"

"He did not say. But he seemed most eager to find you. He asked me if I knew where you were. I told him I thought you had gone up to the Vega for a day or two, deluded foreigner that you are, but I don't think he believed me. He is an unpleasant man, I think."

"I think so, too."

Ali began to fill another urn. Some of the beans ricocheted off the rim and skittered across the mosaic floor. I waited until he was finished, until it was quiet—and it was the sort of hushed, sudden quiet that succeeds a lengthy tintinnabulation—and then I said, "What am I going to do, Ali?"

"What are you going to do about what?"

"About my life."

"Oh, there is nothing to do about that. The less you do the better."

"But everything has gone wrong. I am in trouble."

"With this man Afgroni?" He stood and folded the burlap bag into quarters.

"Yes," I said. "Primarily. I keep making mistakes."

"Then I expect you have gotten what you deserve."

"No," I said. "I don't deserve this."

"It is only in retrospect that you can know that," said Ali.

Inside my apartment with the windows closed, the doors locked, the drapes drawn, I did not feel the world closing in on me—no, I felt it all falling away, as if the seams that held my life together had ripped and everything was slowly tipping and slipping off the horizon. I felt sick and weak, as if my fabricated illness was becoming real and I actually was susceptible to the terrible motion of living.

I lay on the bed and looked up through the wreath of hands. Once you take comfort in something, you foolishly think it will always provide comfort, but now I felt neither blessed nor comforted by the four hands floating above my head. I remembered looking up into the conical ceiling of my room in the Hotel Excelsior, the perfection of that. I should never have left there, I thought. I remembered those first days in Andorra as being happy and golden, but then beginnings always are. Or always seem to be in retrospect.

So much of my life seems to me happy only in retrospect.

But that's not true. I was happy those first days, keenly and sentiently happy.

One day, the summer before Anna was born, Helen and I were at the ocean. We had rented a house in Truro. It was late in the day, but we stayed on the beach, lingered as everyone else left and the sand grew cool. We stayed because we could not bear to leave, because we were happy and we knew it. It seemed like a miracle, I remember, a very simple but fabulous miracle: to be alive and simultaneously happy with another person whom you loved and who loved you, the sort of miracle that could sustain you for a very long time.

Forever, we thought.

I covered my eyes with my hands and tried to cry, tried to transform the tension and sorrow inside myself into tears. But they would not come. I realized that my worst failure was in not sensing my failure sooner. I had been doomed from the very first day; I had arrived in Andorra a failed person and had expected the geography to rehabilitate me.

I wanted to get out of the house before Afgroni returned. I fetched my valise and looked around the room for what to pack, but suddenly all the objects around me seemed unbearably poignant and beloved. It was hard to believe that they really had no intrinsic value or worth: the fantastic bed dragged halfway across the world, the mosaic-topped table out on the patio, the onyx chess-piece lighter, the celadon teacups. And my journal, which lay on Uncle Roderick's desk, the batiked fabric faded now by the sun.

I stuffed some random, useless objects into the valise: the gauze nightshirt, the shaving brush, the tourmaline cuff links, the undershorts with their chased silver buckles. My journal. I knew it was pathetic, but one feels one should pack for a trip, even a trip like the one I was about to take, without a purpose or a destination.

It was just getting dark when I left the house. I locked the door and slipped the key beneath the pot of still-desiccated geraniums. I had always intended to water them, and I had always forgotten.

It was still hours until midnight. I didn't know where to go, so I wandered down through the town, down the darkest and narrowest streets, down the alleys and staircases, down through the silent terraces, the windows shuttered above me, the birds in their bamboo cages all silenced by darkness, just a velvety rustling of wings high above me, down and down, until I found myself in the alley that ran behind the Hotel Excelsior, alongside the ancient Roman wall. I reached out and touched it with my hand, as if to draw strength or wisdom from it. Of course it offered me neither of those things, and I realized it was time for me to stop seeking them in talismans. I liked the wall, though: I felt a little comforted that some things endured, some things didn't collapse and decay as the centuries washed uselessly over them. Yet of course the Roman wall was decaying; in fact, my touching it hastened its decay. I laid my cheek and then my forehead against the Roman wall, and I thought of the Wailing Wall, and then I thought: Jesus wept. Why did Jesus weep? I knew He wept toward the end when things were going badly for Him, but what was it, I wondered, that finally moved Him to tears? For the first time I felt that I understood, on a simple human level, the drama of Jesus, the simple downward-spiraling narrative, the betrayal leading to betrayal, down and down until up He rose.

I stood back and looked at the Hotel Excelsior. From behind, it looked a little ugly: its stuccoed façade unadorned save for pipes and gutters and cables, its rear windows small and mean with bright light. Yet it looked a good place to hide, and I liked the idea of spending my last hours in Andorra where I had spent my first. Symmetry is, by definition, comforting.

I entered through an unmarked service door and climbed up dank fire stairs as far as I could go, exhausting myself. I opened the door onto a dark low-ceilinged uncarpeted hallway. I was up in the attics, I realized, beneath the eaves. It smelled of dust and age, a sort of stale public warmth. The doors along the hall were all closed except for one, which was open into a room crowded with furniture, rolled carpets, and stacks of books. There was one small grimy window, shaped like a fanlight, at the level of the floor, and I made my way through the maze of stacked furniture to a safe corner behind a huge chifforobe, whose doors were inlaid with garlands of fruitwood and mother-of-pearl. I sat down on the wide planks of the floor and closed my eyes. I could feel the self-contented hive of the hotel below me, all the many floors of it swarming with life, with people bathing or fucking or sleeping or dressing for dinner. The silent windowless corridors that stayed lit all night long, year after year, through blizzards and thunderstorms, like corridors in a prison, as seasonless as the bottom of the ocean.

It occurred to me that perhaps I was wrong to panic. I opened my eyes. What if Afgroni had come to bring me good news? Perhaps the real murderer had been caught and he was coming to absolve me and return my passport. How else to explain his haste? Why else would he seek me out so soon after our interview?

Ali's impression of Afgroni was not that of a man bearing good news. Yet Ali was not well attuned to felicity; he saw evil and failure in everything, so I could not trust his response. Perhaps Afgroni had come to liberate me. I would never know.

Beside me on the floor was a tall pile of books, and I could see in the gloom that the book on the top of the pile was a Bible. Its black leather boards were dried and peeling, and pieces of them flaked off as I touched it. *Jesus wept.* I thought it was in John, and I squatted on the floor in the dim light and tried to find the shortest verse in the Bible.

Did He weep in the garden? Or on the cross at Golgotha? No— no. I couldn't find *Jesus wept* anywhere in John. I began to look through the other books, Matthew, Mark, Luke, scanning and turning the tissuey pages. But there was no weeping Jesus in them either. Or none that I could find. Perhaps *Jesus wept* wasn't in the Bible in the way that *Play it again, Sam* wasn't really in *Casablanca*. Nevertheless, I felt a little cheated that I had looked to the Bible for help and it had offered me none.

Then I saw: *Jesus wept.* The two words staked by periods. It was much earlier on in John than I had thought it would be: Jesus wept at the tomb of Lazarus before He raised him from the dead. Jesus wept because He loved Lazarus. And He raised him from the dead. And I felt a little ashamed that I had assumed Jesus wept over His own travails, that He had wept when things got bad for Himself, but He hadn't. He had wept for someone else.

As I closed the book I noticed that there was an inscription on the flyleaf:

> To Lucille Guinevere Houck
> presented to her
> on the occasion of her first Holy Communion
> by the congregation of St. Sabina's Parish Church
> on the 6th day of May 1906

> *I think of God, and I moan;*
> *I meditate and my spirit faints.*
> *Thou dost hold my eyelids from closing;*
> *I am so troubled that I cannot speak.*
> —*Psalms 77: 3–4*

I replaced the Bible on the top of the pile of books. It was then that I sensed I was not alone. I stood up as quietly as I could and peered around the side of the chifforobe. A figure was standing in the gloom by the door, and for a few moments it just stood there, surveying the jumbled contents of the room. A woman. And then she entered the room, walking slowly and hesitantly, like a blind person, holding her hands out before her to protect herself. As she neared the window, I saw that it was Mrs. Reinhardt. I stepped out from behind the chifforobe and quietly said her name.

She stopped walking and turned toward me. "Who is it?" she asked.

I stepped closer to her. "It's me," I said. "Alexander Fox."

"Mr. Fox!" she exclaimed. "What are you doing up here?"

"Hiding," I said.

"Hiding? From whom?"

"From the police," I said.

"The police? Whatever for?"

"They think I am a murderer," I said.

For a moment she said nothing. She remained standing where she was. "How odd life is," she said, almost to herself. "How very odd."

"Yes," I said. "What are you doing up here?"

"I heard a noise and came up here to check my things," she said.

"These are your things?"

"Yes," she said. "But not for much longer."

"Why?"

"They're to be auctioned," she said. "Everything. To pay for my room and board. You see, I've lost my suite. And now I shall lose all my things."

"Why?"

"My life estate expired. Can you imagine? Apparently in Andorra a life estate is only good for fifty years. I suppose at the time I agreed to it, I never imagined I'd live this long."

"And where are you living now?"

"Oh, they have not turned me out on the street. They've given me a maid's room, on the floor just below us. It's very snug." She reached out and touched a chiffonnier, slaloming her finger through the dust. "I suppose it's the price you pay for living too long. I don't advise it."

I said nothing.

"And for how long have you been hiding in the attic?" she asked.

"An hour or two. At midnight I'll leave, and try to get away."

"How romantic you are: escaping at midnight. Where will you go?"

"To France, I think."

"Ah," said Mrs. Reinhardt, "France. All the more romantic, still. Did you know I lived in Paris before the war? There wasn't a more beautiful place on earth. Will you go to Paris?"

"I don't know," I said.

"If you do, think of me there. Think of me in Paris. I was young in Paris. And in love. It's where I met Hervé. In fact, you must take something with you. It would give me great pleasure to know that something of mine has escaped with a friend to Paris, and not been sold to strangers." She looked about the room, at the chifforobe, the mute lyre-back chairs lined up against a wall, the four-hundred-day clock. "What would you like?" she asked. "What can I give you?"

"Nothing," I said. "I'm afraid I'm not bringing anything with me."

"But you must have something," she said. "For my sake, take something, please. Something small that you can carry with you." She opened one of the drawers of the chiffonnier and felt inside it. "Here," she said, holding something out to me. "It's Hervé's

Freemason ring. I want you to have it. You aren't a Mason, are you?"

"No," I said. "I'm not."

"I suppose no one is anymore. See if it fits you. He had such small hands, Hervé did. Like a boy's. Beautiful hands."

The ring was too small for my ring finger, but it fit snugly on my pinky. It was a handsome ring: gold, with a lapis-lazuli stone.

"Yes," she said, "wear it there. Wear it in health and happiness."

"Thank you very much," I said. "I will treasure it."

"I'm glad you'll have it. Is there anything else you'd like? Books, perhaps?"

"Actually, I was just looking at your Bible," I said.

"My Bible? I did not know I still had one."

"Yes," I said. "It's behind the chifforobe." I went and got it. I showed it to her and then read the inscription.

"Ah yes," she said. "Do you know, I actually remember that day. It was my first great disappointment. You see, my mother told me it would be the most wonderful day of my life: the day I finally took Christ's body into my own. She said I would see angels and feel the presence of God. And of course I saw and felt nothing. I felt so cheated, so betrayed. I never forgave my mother, or really trusted her again after that. She was a bit of a religious hysteric, I later realized. A sweet woman, but a little too much in love with God. My father was agnostic. Are you a religious man?"

"No," I said. "I'm afraid I am not."

"Yet you are a good man," she said. "Like my father. Such a good, kind man he was. When we were in the country he would go out before breakfast and say hello to all the animals. Every morning, in all weather. How he loved his horses! He would come into breakfast smelling of them. I can still remember that smell. Well. That's all long ago and far away, isn't it?" She looked at me. She looked triumphant rather than pathetic. How hard it is to come to the end of your life, I thought. But how wonderful if you can come there with dignity.

I was still holding the Bible.

"Would you like the Bible?" she asked me. "You may take it if you want."

"May I?"

"Of course," she said. "It's sad not to have family to give things to. It makes it absurd to have things, in fact. All this, all these things I love, become absurd. I didn't realize that until they were brought up here, but once I was separated from them, I realized how little they really mean to me. I think I shall be relieved to see them go. Goodbye to all that." She made a dismissive gesture with her hand. "Well, I suppose if you are hiding from the police I should leave you be. How unpleasant for you. Is there anything you need? Are you thirsty, perhaps? Would you like some tea? I have an electric kettle in my room."

"No, thank you," I said.

"Then I will leave," she said. "But I am so glad I saw you again. God speed, Mr. Fox."

"The same to you," I said.

"Yes," she said. "I hope my next voyage is a swift and peaceful one. Good night."

"Good night," I said. I shook her hand, and watched her disappear back into the gloom of the hallway. I heard her light tread in the hall, and then everything was quiet, save for the four-hundred-day clock, ticking itself to death inside its glass dome.

As I crossed the plaza at midnight the fountain ceased cascading and went dark, like some insect folding up its glorious incandescent wings. I glanced up at the turret of the Hotel Excelsior. My room—the room that had been mine—was lighted and I could see the curtains blowing in and out of the open balcony doors. And a figure standing at the railing, looking down, with proprietary smugness, at the small glittering world. He had probably just arrived.

It was Vere, not Jean, who awaited me in the alley outside the cantina. I could tell by the nervous way he greeted me that meeting people in alleys at midnight was not something he often did. "Jean's told me everything," he said. "We decided it would be easier for me to get you aboard the *Splendora*, since I know the crew."

I followed him around to the front of the cantina. Most of the tables were empty, but a few people still lingered beneath the umbrellas, leaning in toward one another over their iced bottles of wine, their faces warmed by candlelight, and I thought, How lucky they are and they do not know it, or even suspect it. It is hard to believe that life goes on and on for some people, golden and uninterrupted, a bolt of beautiful cloth endlessly unraveling. I was aware that I was seeing everything for the last time, and I felt panicked, for I suddenly realized I could imagine no reality for myself after Andorra.

We walked down the steps and along the promenade, out onto the seawall. The water was dark and laced with spume. It smelled a little unpleasantly of fish and petrol. The entrance to the marina was at the far end of the jetty, and a little shack stood beside the gangway that led down onto the floating decks. A policeman sat in this shack, beneath a hanging lightbulb, reading a pornographic comic book. The bulb cast forth a little pool of light, and as we approached it, he stopped us merely by looking up. "I need to see your passports," he said.

I felt too stupid to say anything. I am going to be executed, was all I thought. Vere said something to the man about our only going aboard to get something off a boat. The man repeated, as if he had not heard Vere, that he needed to see our passports. Vere showed him his passport. The guard looked at me. I stepped back into the shadows. I haven't got my passport, I said. Then you cannot enter the marina, the guard said. He returned his attention to the comic book. He wetted his finger and turned a page.

Vere walked a way down the seawall, back toward the promenade, and made a motion for me to follow him. Listen, he said to me. Are you listening?

Yes, I said. I was trying to listen, but something about the policeman reading a comic book enraged me: that an illiterate should be in control of my future.

I'm going back, said Vere, and I'm going to get on the boat. I'll wake the captain and have him take the *Splendora* around the point and out a way. Go back to Quayside. Can you swim?

Yes, I said.

Are you a good swimmer?

I told him I was.

Wait on the beach. When you see the boat—it will have a blue light on it—swim out to it. That's the only way I can think to get you on board. We don't want to risk anything here. Do you understand? We'll come as close to land as we can, but it may be quite far. You're not drunk, are you?

No, I said.

All right, he said. He reached out and clutched my arm, just above my elbow. He shook it a little roughly. Go now, he said. It shouldn't take long.

The peninsula road was like a road in a dream: straight, dark, and eerily quiet, the ancient trees standing sentinel along either verge. The gates of Quayside were closed. The metal latch was cool, and the gate rasped against the gravel. I closed it behind me and walked across the lawn. The darkness had carefully leached all the color from the rhododendron and hydrangea blossoms. The house was all dark save for a gas lantern beneath the porte cochere and a few lighted rooms on the upper floors. As I crossed the lawn toward the cliff, I tripped over a forgotten boccie ball which rested, like a huge black pearl, on the grass.

On the beach I stood and waited, scouring the sea, as if I wouldn't see the blue light. When it appeared it seemed very far away. Farther than I had ever swum. I still clutched my little valise stuffed with foolishness. And Mrs. Reinhardt's Bible. I hadn't thought to give my valise to Vere, and I knew I couldn't swim with it. I put it down on the rocks and took off my clothes and folded them carefully across the top of the bag. I waded out as far as I could, and then tried to wade farther, but the land fell away beneath my feet, and I shivered, and began to swim in the direction of the blue light. Almost immediately I encountered a cold current, and the farther out I swam, the stronger it got, pulling me away from the boat. I felt a fish rise up and brush against me, glancing, gelatinous, and I tried not to panic. I concentrated on swimming, but the blue light refused to grow, it sat stubbornly in the distance, and every time I stopped to look, it seemed to have shrunk. They've given up, I thought, and they're sailing away from me, returning to the marina. I swam faster, and the next time I looked up I could see the boat as well as the light, and then I looked up every 100 strokes, and each time the boat was larger, and finally I touched it, the beautiful white skin of it, and Vere threw down a rope ladder, which I managed to climb with my last bit of strength.

I was panting and shivering and I vomited a geyser of seawater over the side of the boat. I stood there a moment, steadying myself against the railing, my head lowered, and then I looked up, back at the shore, and it almost broke my heart, the view of Andorra from the sea by moonlight. The dark verdant arm of the peninsula reaching out into the sea, and behind it the town rising up the side of the hill in its concentric rings, the red granite blanched the palest pink by the moon. And above La Plata the sheer dark cliff, on the top of which glittered the few lights of forsaken Encampo. I stood at the railing, trying to regain my breath, and then the boat started to move and Vere said we should go down below, and I turned away from it all and did not look back: I followed Vere down below to a little windowless cabin. He brought me a towel and pajamas, and I suddenly remembered my clothes and my valise, abandoned on the pebbly shore. I asked Vere if he would collect them for me and bring them in the morning.

He said that he would.

I rubbed myself with the towel and put on the pajamas and got into bed. I could feel the motor and hear the dark water shushing against the thin wall. I started to shake again and I couldn't stop. Vere brought me a large brandy. I drank it and felt a calm warmth begin to spread foggily through my body. Vere stood beside the bed, the empty glass of brandy in his hand. I waited for him to say something, but he said nothing. I wanted to ask him why he was helping me, but I couldn't think of a way of asking that wouldn't arouse his suspicions. He reached out and turned off the light, but remained standing there, in the light from the open door, watching me watch him.

I woke in darkness, a perfect darkness that seemed to be both outside and inside me, a darkness I had trouble distinguishing myself from in a way that was almost comforting. I thought: This is what death is like.

Then there was a sudden bright brief stripe of light in the darkness, and I realized a door had been opened and hurriedly closed and that someone was in the dark room with me.

The someone stood in the room for a moment, as if allowing the darkness to resettle and perfect itself, and then said, "Are you awake?" It was Miss Quay.

"Yes," I said.

I heard her feel her way toward the bed. She sat beside it. "How do you feel?" she asked.

"All right," I said. "Tired. A little disoriented. Where are we?"

"You're safe. We're about an hour or two away from Andorra. Everything's fine."

"Good," I said. "Thank you."

"Well," she said, "maybe not everything. Listen, something's happened. Mother went down to the beach this morning to stow her kayak and found your clothes and bag."

"I asked Vere to get them."

"I know. He planned to, this morning, but Mother was up before anyone. She insisted we call the police. Of course, Vere and I tried to dissuade her, but under the circumstances there was little we could do without giving everything away. And then we thought perhaps it was all for the best."

"What?"

She said nothing.

"What?" I asked again. "What was for the best?"

"For everyone to think you had killed yourself. That you are dead."

"Is that what they think?"

"Yes. It's certainly how things looked. Of course, the police are waiting to find your body. But it could wash ashore anywhere, or not at all, so I don't think it matters. You are assumed dead, as far as Andorra is concerned."

I said nothing.

"It's probably all for the best," said Miss Quay. "Don't you think?" She reached out her hand and found my forehead in the dark. I remembered her touching Bitsy's forehead in the same way. "You're a little warm," she said. "Do you feel as though you have a fever?"

"Yes," I said.

"I'll bring you some aspirin."

"Does your mother think that I am dead?"

"Yes. That's why we'll have to be careful getting you off the boat. She and Isolta mustn't see you. We're stopping overnight quite near the coast and we'll row you to shore at dawn. It shouldn't take long."

"In France?"

"Yes. I think it will be somewhere near Marseille. I've got to go now. I've brought you down a sandwich and some fruit and bottled water. I'm putting them here, beside the bed. The bottle's open, so be careful. The toilet's next door, if you need it. Just make sure no one is about. Is there anything else I can get you?"

"No," I said. "Thank you."

She sat there for a moment. I was just beginning to be able to discern the surface of her face in the darkness: the slight luminosity of her skin and eyes. "Yesterday, at the gate. You said you wanted to tell me something and I stopped you. Do you still wish to tell me something?"

I knew it was my last chance, but it seemed too late. "No," I said.

She stood. "Then I will leave you. I won't come back down. Vere will come for you in the morning."

"What about you?"

"I think it would be better if Vere and you went alone. It would attract less attention."

"Come," I said. "Please come."

I could tell she was standing by the door.

"You've been so kind to me, always. Please do this last thing. If I leave without you, it will seem so sad."

For a long moment it was quiet and I thought that perhaps she had snuck out somehow. "Are you still there?" I asked.

"Yes," she said.

I waited.

"May I ask you a question?" she said.

"Yes," I said.

"Did you kill them?"

For a moment I said nothing. I looked up into the darkness, and it was the darkness, I think, the not being able to see her, or anything, that allowed me to say yes.

"Why?"

People always want to know why, as if there is a reason. As if when you are throttling someone you are thinking rationally, when really you are not thinking at all, you have gone somewhere terrible beyond thinking and you are doing it because it is the only thing left you can do. "Because it seemed at the moment the only thing to do," I said. "It seemed necessary, inevitable. It was like stopping something that had to be stopped."

"But I don't understand. Why those men? Why in that ghastly way? What were you trying to stop?"

"What men?" I asked.

"The men in the harbor," she said.

"I didn't kill the men in the harbor," I said. "Why would I kill the men in the harbor?"

"But you just said you did. You told me you did."

"No," I said. "You misunderstood me."

She was silent a moment, and then she said, "Who did you kill?"

I could go back, if I wanted to. I could take it all back and be safe again. But I would never be safe again. Helen walking across the field toward me with tears in her eyes and leaves in her hair —

"Tell me," said Miss Quay. She said it gently. "Don't not tell me."

"I killed my wife," I said. "And my daughter."

She made no sound at all. Miss Quay: standing there in her dress, in the darkness, clutching the doorknob behind her back.

"Why?" she asked.

Why?

Because she stopped loving me. Because she loved someone else. Because she said she never really loved me. Because she laughed at me. Because she didn't want to touch me anymore. Or me to touch her. Because she wouldn't let me hold the baby. Because she turned away from me in the night. Because I have never liked myself. Because she opened a separate bank account. Because she started calling the baby Annie instead of Anna. Because she told me the baby wasn't really mine. Because she wanted to leave me. Because she told the pond man to dredge the pond, to make it deep, really deep, deep enough for someone to drown themselves in. Because she sold the signed first edition of *In Youth Is Pleasure* for ten bucks.

And Anna? Because she had seen it all, and even though they say babies don't remember, I knew, from the way she looked at me, that she would. She would always remember, always remind me. And so I killed her, too, because I did not have the wits to kill myself.

"I cannot explain it to you," I said.

"No," she said. "I suppose not."

There was a long silence.

"Will you come tomorrow?" I finally asked.

"Yes," said Miss Quay. "I will come." And then she opened the door, and closed it behind her.

When Vere rowed us ashore in the morning the sun had risen and it was already warm, yet everything was quiet and still and asleep; the boat, the water, the whole world. None of us spoke. Just the sound of the oars displacing the water and the creak of the oarlocks. Miss Quay sat in the prow and turned her face away from me, over her shoulder, watching the shore come close.

There was no beach, just a stretch of shallow rocky water and a boulder-studded embankment. Vere managed to steer the dinghy through the rocks into a still pool of water at the edge of the embankment. Miss Quay climbed out onto a pebbly shoal; Vere and I stepped into the water and pulled the boat up onto the rocks. We stood there for a moment, looking up and down the embankment. It was too tall to climb.

"It looks as though if you walked around the edge down there, you could climb up," said Miss Quay. It was the first thing anyone had said since they had come to wake me. "It isn't half as steep as it is here."

"Yes," said Vere. "That seems the only place."

I could not move or speak.

After a moment Miss Quay said, "Come, and I will come with you. Do we have time, Vere?"

Vere looked at his watch. "Yes," he said. "I'll wait here."

Miss Quay took my arm and said, "Come." We began to walk along the wet, rocky shoal, at the base of the embankment, toward where the slope was more gentle. We did not speak. We went quite far — perhaps a quarter of a mile — before we encountered a place where we could climb up onto the bank. We found ourselves in a grassy field beside a dirt road. There was a burnt spot where a fire had been. On the opposite side of the road were terraces of olive trees. There were no buildings in sight.

We stood there looking up and down the road.

"Well," said Miss Quay, "which way will you go?"

"I don't know," I said.

"I suppose there is a town in either direction," she said. "And from the town I am sure it will be no trouble getting to Paris. So I shall leave you here. I hope it all works out for you, and that—"

"Come with me," I said.

She was silent. For a moment I thought perhaps I hadn't said it, only thought it.

But then she said, "What do you mean?"

"Don't leave me now."

"I can't come with you," said Miss Quay.

"Why not?" I asked.

"I can't," she said. "It's not something I can do."

"I love you," I said.

She looked at me. "Do you?" she said. She looked back toward the boat, but it was hidden beneath the embankment. Then she shook her head, ever so slightly. "I don't think you do. I think you think you love me because you are scared of going on alone. But that is what you must do."

"I love you," I said. "I am sure of it."

"I am not," she said.

"What can I say to convince you?"

"Nothing," she said.

"Do you love me?"

"I don't know. I've thought I do, some moments. But I don't know."

"But you may."

"I may. Yes, it is possible: I may."

"Then come with me. Do you remember what you told me about Ceylon? How you lost your chance there?"

"Of course I do. And of course I think of that now. But—"

"But what?"

"It was different, what happened in Ceylon. I should have gone with him, yes. I'll always regret that I did not. But this is different."

"How?"

"How? I trusted him. I trusted him completely. I could imagine nothing but happiness with him. And it is not the same with you. I don't trust you completely, I can imagine . . ."

"What?"

"I can imagine unhappiness with you."

"But can you imagine happiness?"

"Yes," she said. "But not enough to walk down this road with you. I'm sorry. I know I've failed you. And perhaps I've failed myself. But—well. That is what happens in life. And now I should go back to Vere. I've been too long."

I said nothing.

She looked at the road and then pointed in one direction. "I think you should go this way," she said.

"Then that is the way I will go," I said.

She stood there. The breeze picked up some strands of her hair, which was gathered, as always, at the back of her head.

"Will you do me a favor?" I asked her.

"What?"

"Take down your hair," I said. "I have never seen you with your hair let down."

She narrowed her eyes a little, and then reached a hand up to her bun and drew the pins from it. Her hair fell down her back in a long, thin coil. She shook her head a little in an unsuccessful attempt to loosen it. I reached out and touched her hair. She closed her eyes. I drew my fingers through the length of it, and then let it fall back in place. She looked very different with her hair down: older and a little pathetic.

After a moment she opened her eyes and stepped away from me. She wound her hair back up and stuck it with pins. She looked like herself again.

"Thank you," I said. "Thank you for all you have done."

"Will you write to me?" she asked.

"Yes," I said.

"Then I shan't say goodbye. I will only say good luck. Be well." And she turned and scrambled down the embankment to the shore. I stepped up to the edge and watched her walk along the shoal. She did not look back. The tide was rising and in places she had to jump from rock to rock. I watched her get in the little boat, watched it row out to the *Splendora*. I did not want to leave until the *Splendora* had left, so I waited there, sitting on the bluff. I suppose I thought—or hoped—that she might change her mind, decide to come with me after all, and I would see the little boat rowing back toward the shore. And she would come running toward me through the shallow pools of water. I sat and waited. As the sun rose it got warmer. I lay down on the warm earth. I looked up at the cloudless sky. How blue it was.

When I sat up the *Splendora* was moving away from me, quickly, it seemed, as if it was in a hurry to be gone. And then it was gone, and the sea was perfectly empty, and the *Splendora* was gone in such a way as to suggest that it might never have been there. I sat there for a long time, looking out at the blank expanse of the sea.

How quickly things disappear.

It is as quiet as it ever gets. The fluorescent light in my cell flickers off. Midnight. I suppose I have to face the fact that my book is finished and I am not. Yet I go on writing in the darkness, writing because I cannot bear to stop. Just words, the gushing nonstop vocabulary of the world: lattice, footlight, amphora, gesticulate, séance, clasp, winnow, Constantinople, cyclical, leveret, basenji, chalice, jackdaw. Geraniums. Floating market.

Gramophone, Euphrosyne, penultimate. Millicent Sherwood. Cocktail.

Andorra. Many years ago I read a book that was set in Andorra . . .